First published in Great Britain in 2012 by Simon and Schuster UK Ltd,
a CBS company.
Simon & Schuster UK Ltd
1st Floor, 222 Gray's Inn Road, London WC1X 8HB

www.simonandschuster.co.uk
www.markgriffithsbooks.co.uk

Text copyright © Mark Griffiths 2012
Illustrations copyright © Peter Williamson 2012
Design by Jane Buckley

A CIP catalogue record for this book is available from the British Library.

PB ISBN: 978-0-85707-132-3
eBook ISBN: 978-0-85707-888-9

1 3 5 7 9 10 8 6 4 2

Printed in the UK by CPI Cox and Wyman Ltd,
Reading, Berkshire RG1 8EX

MARK GRIFFITHS

illustrated by
Pete Williamson

SPACE LIZARDS
ATE MY SISTER!

SIMON AND SCHUSTER

FOR JO

With thanks to Kate at the Viney Agency,
Jane G, Jane B and Kat at Simon & Schuster,
Pete Williamson, Pete Wallis, Matt Hill and Nick Devereux.

PROLOGUE

SHHH TOP SECRET

PASSWORD

PET'S NAME

FAVOURITE MILKSHAKE

PICK UP YOUR TOP SECRET
UK GOVERNMENT WELCOME PACK
FROM
WWW.DON'TTELLANYONEITSASECRET.CO.UK

A pair of long, green claws danced over the buttons of a mobile phone. It was a very new, very complicated kind of mobile phone, the sort that lets you send emails or tells you what the weather is going to be like in Cardiff tomorrow, should you wish to know that sort of thing.

The owner of the claws was using the phone

to surf the Internet.

In fact, the owner of the claws was using it to access a top-secret website owned by the UK Government. The site was not normally accessible to the general public, hidden as it was behind many layers of encryption, firewalls, passwords and other forms of electronic protection, but one of the things the owner of the claws also owned was a mind of subtle and fiendish genius, and it found sidestepping the site's security measures as easy as opening an envelope.

A list of documents appeared on the phone's screen. A spindly green finger scrolled through it.

The documents were ranked in secrecy from Reasonably Confidential (Try not to leave on the train if you can help it, please)

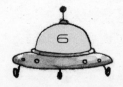

to Ultra-Ultra-Top-Really-Awfully-Tip-Top-Top-Secret-Indeed (Breathe a word of this to anyone and you are toast, mate). The spindly green finger selected a document from this latter category and double-clicked on it. Another thing that the owner of the claws also owned was a pair of small, cunning eyes and it now used these to read the startling words that had just materialised on the screen before it.

THE COTTLETON INCIDENT

Report for the Prime Minister prepared by the Secret Service (Bizarre Incidents Division).

The recent extraordinary events in Cottleton are only now beginning to be understood. The following is the most complete account of what happened that we can currently compile and is based on interviews with those directly involved.

On the fifteenth of October last year, what was initially thought to be a meteorite fell to Earth just outside the small town of Cottleton (population: 12,022; principal industry: the manufacture of desk tidies). The meteorite was in fact a sophisticated piece of alien technology - an information storage device not dissimilar to a computer's hard disk or a USB stick, only with a staggeringly vaster memory capacity. Stored on the device was the brain pattern of an alien creature called Admiral Skink, the self-styled grand ruler of a savage and warlike race of reptiles known as the Swerdlixian Lizard Swarm. This information storage device was found by two schoolchildren, Lance Uriah Marwood Percival Spratley of 55 Mercer Road, Cottleton and Victoria Madonna Walnut of Ark Villas, Binturong Avenue, Cottleton. Admiral Skink's brain pattern took over and inhabited the body of said Lance Spratley and, by cleverly obtaining the necessary components from an internet auction site, assembled an energy weapon of devastating power. Some freak mishap with this weapon caused a triceratops skull in the local museum to spontaneously grow into a living, breathing dinosaur, which

Admiral Skink then rode around the town, causing an estimated two and three-quarter million pounds worth of damage to buildings and other property. It seems the memory device on which Admiral Skink's mind had been stored also contained a homing beacon that was leading a fleet of spaceships towards our planet with the express purpose of enslaving and/or blowing up everyone on it. A timely intervention from the young Walnut and Spratley (whose own brain pattern had been imprisoned within the memory device while Admiral Skink used his body), coupled with the assistance of a local policeman, PC Sledge, saved the day, removing the evil intelligence of

Admiral Skink from the body of Lance Spratley and confining it within the body of a common iguana. This iguana is now held captive in a special vivarium housed within the basement of Cottleton's police station, where PC Sledge acts as Admiral Skink's jailer. The triceratops was adopted by Cottleton Museum, where it became for a short time the subject of great publicity (although strangely most people believe it to be an animatronic fake, despite the two-metre-tall piles of dung it deposits in its enclosure every day).

PERSONAL STATEMENT #1
LANCE SPRATLEY

'Space lizards stole my brain! That was incredible! And then a dinosaur smashed up my house! How insane is that? And then my family got turned into jellies and then reassembled into people! Completely freaky or what, eh? Other than that it was a normal couple of days.'

PERSONAL STATEMENT #2
VICTORIA 'TORI' WALNUT

'It's amazing to think that we saved the entire world from invasion and destruction at the hands of an evil race of alien lizards! I suppose Lance and I are due a huge reward and we're going to become mega-celebrities? What do you mean you'll have to hush it all up in the interests of "national security"? That's so not fair!'

PERSONAL STATEMENT #3
PC SLEDGE

'Between you and me I'm glad all this lizard and dinosaur stuff happened. Cottleton really lacked what I call "pizzazz" and I was so bored being a policeman that I nearly gave it all up to work in a pet shop. I bet that's a right laugh!'

PERSONAL STATEMENT #4
ADMIRAL SKINK

'I have nothing to say to you wretched apes. Buzz off.'

CONCLUSION

Although currently captive, we believe Admiral Skink remains extremely dangerous. It had been suggested we move him to a higher-security facility to study him and to try to obtain the secrets of his advanced alien culture, but the fact is he gives everyone the creeps and we're perfectly happy for him to stay in Cottleton, thank you very much.

ULTRA ⚡ PHONE

Admiral Skink switched off the mobile phone with a flick of his long iguana claw. The screen went black. He gave a snort of satisfaction. Stealing the phone from PC Sledge as he was reaching into the vivarium to change the gravel had been pathetically easy, but no

doubt the policeman would soon notice that it was missing and retrace his steps. So what to do with it in the meantime? Order the components of another super weapon over the internet? Track down Lance Spratley and Tori Walnut? Prank call PC Sledge's mother?

Maybe.

Admiral Skink yawned and settled himself comfortably beneath the vivarium's ultraviolet lamp. He closed his eyes and let the mobile phone flop on to the gravel.

He was in no hurry. When the right moment came, he would know what to do.

And when it did, the entire human race would pay the consequences.

CHAPTER ONE
FUNSTRONOMY

'No one, absolutely no one, is having ice cream. Is that understood?'

Twenty-five children howled like a pack of very disappointed wolves.

'I'm sorry,' said Mr Taylor. 'But it's a waste of money. It makes you fat. It's terrible for your teeth. It gets everywhere. And all the sugar in it turns you lot into hyperactive idiots. It is in

my experience the number one cause of ill-discipline on school trips. So there will be no ice cream today. For anyone. In fact the entire café in the visitor centre is out of bounds. They have scones there too and they're almost as bad.'

'But sir—!'

'But sir nothing!' said Mr Taylor and mimed zipping up his mouth.

Twenty-five faces scowled back at him.

He turned to the strange little man standing next to him. The man was wearing oversized glasses and a flowing cape made of sparkly material. On his head was a large spherical hat painted to look like a weird alien planet, complete with a system of cardboard rings. 'Sorry for that interruption, Doctor Planetnoggin, please continue.'

17

'Sure thing, dude!' said the little man. He had the kind of voice you would more usually expect to belong to a cartoon rabbit rather than a human being. 'OK, my fellow funstronomers! We've had a totally, totally fun time so far, haven't we? We saw the film in the visitor centre about the history of the observatory and that was totally, totally fun! Then we saw the exhibition showing the relative sizes of the planets in the solar system and that was totally, totally fun too! Now we're going to go up to the main telescope and take a look at the sky! What's that going to be, dudes?' He cupped his hand to his ear expectantly.

'Totally, totally boring?' said a girl's voice. The class sniggered.

'Oi!' said Mr Taylor. 'Watch it, Jasmine!'

'It was Peach!' protested Jasmine. Peach and Jasmine were a pair of straggle-haired girls whose principal interests in life were pointing out why things were rubbish and then smirking.

'Whoever it was,' said Mr Taylor, 'just shut it. Righto. Lead the way, Doctor . . . thingy.'

'Sure thing, dude,' cried Doctor Planetnoggin. 'This way, funstronomers!' He scampered up some concrete steps that wound their way up the hill towards the metal dome of the observatory. The children trudged after him, sighing and grumbling. The steps were steep and narrow and there were an awful lot of them.

'Funstronomy,' muttered Tori Walnut, looking at her best friend, Lance Spratley, through her unruly mop of curly hair, as they

19

climbed the steps. 'Have you ever heard of anything so daft? You won't get airheads like Peach and Jasmine interested in a subject just by adding the word "fun" to its name. It's Quadratic Funquations all over again.'

Lance and Tori were the sole members of a club devoted to science, computers and arguing over the club's name (Lance favoured Knowledge Warriors, Tori Knowledge Champions). Some of their classmates had come up with their own names for the club behind their backs – names like Team Loser, Nerd Patrol, The Unpopular Squad and The League of Extraordinary Swots. But then they didn't know that Lance and Tori had recently saved the entire world from destruction by Admiral Skink and his scaly alien hordes.

'Manchester City,' said Lance, pointing at a boy in his class. He pointed at three more boys in turn. 'Apples, elephants, Timmy the Seasick Wasp.' He chuckled to himself.

'Is there some reason why you're pointing at people and saying random words?' said Tori. 'Or has the thrill of being in an actual observatory affected your brain?'

'Passwords,' replied Lance.

'Come again?'

'You know how we all have a password to log on to the school network?'

'You've stolen everyone's computer password?' said Tori, her eyes widening. 'What are you now, Lance? An identity thief?'

'Not stolen,' said Lance with a grin. 'Guessed.'

'What? How?'

'I have this theory, you see. I reckon most people use their favourite thing as their password. So I did an experiment.' He pointed to the four boys again. 'Everyone knows Owen there is a massive Manchester City fan. Danny likes apples. He must eat about five a day. Elliot is very keen on elephants. And Ben there is absolutely bonkers about a book called *Timmy the Seasick Wasp*. So I tried logging in to the network as each of them using their favourite things as passwords. And you know what? It worked.'

'And what does that prove?'

'Two things,' said Lance. 'The first is that people need to think harder about online security.'

'And the second?'

'That Ben seriously needs to read another

book. *Timmy the Seasick Wasp* is for preschool kids.'

At the top of the steps Doctor Planetnoggin led the children through a door into the observatory. Above them the domed metal roof rose like the ceiling of a cathedral. Dominating the space was a huge metal cylinder. It was surrounded by banks of computers, monitor screens and other equipment.

'Now that,' said Lance, 'is what I call a telescope! Wowee!'

'Totally, totally fun, huh?' said Doctor Planetnoggin. He tapped a key on one of the computers. There was a clanking and whirring noise and the domed roof over the telescope slowly slid open, revealing a stripe of blue-grey evening sky and a single

brilliantly bright star. 'That star you can see up there is actually the planet Venus, dudes. Who wants to come and take a peek at it through the eyepiece?'

Lance and Tori's hands shot up like rockets.

'No, let someone else look first,' said Mr Taylor. 'You two are always first to volunteer for everything.' He scanned the faces of the other children. 'You, Peach. Hop to it.'

Peach rolled her eyes as if she'd just been handed a week's worth of detention and stomped over to the eyepiece at the base of the enormous telescope. Her friend Jasmine smirked.

'Look through it and tell us what you see, dude,' said Doctor Planetnoggin to Peach. 'Go ahead. It's gonna be totally, totally fun!'

Peach sighed and peered through the

eyepiece. 'Your telescope's broken,' she said with a snort. 'I can see two stars, not one.'

'Are you sure?' said Doctor Planetnoggin. 'You should only be able to see one object – the planet Venus.'

Peach shrugged. 'Well I can see two. See for yourself.' She stood aside. Doctor Planetnoggin squinted into the telescope, fiddling with the focus control. Then his jaw fell open.

'I can't quite believe what I'm seeing,' he gasped. 'I thought maybe the telescope was out of focus and you were seeing a double image. But it's not. There really is a new star – or planet, or something – in the sky near Venus. How totally, totally fun!'

'Could it be a meteor?' asked Lance. He and Tori exchanged a startled glance. The last 'meteor' they'd encountered had contained the brain pattern of an evil alien warlord who had been intent on taking over the world, so now they were a little suspicious of unknown rocks flying through space.

'Most probably an asteroid,' said Doctor Planetnoggin. 'A huge lump of rock in orbit around the sun just like the Earth and the other planets. Hmmm . . . ' He tapped a few keys on the nearest computer. 'There aren't

any asteroids scheduled to be this close to the Earth for quite some time. This might be a new discovery!'

'Hey Peach! You've discovered a new space thing!' called Jasmine.

Peach rolled her eyes again. 'Don't tell anyone. They'll think I'm a total geek like Spratley or Walnut Whip over there.'

Lance opened his mouth to respond but Tori clamped her hand over it. 'Could the asteroid be heading for Earth?' she asked.

Doctor Planetnoggin gave a little chuckle. 'The chances of that are extremely remote, dude. Here at the observatory we're actually part of a network of telescopes that monitor all known near-Earth asteroids and if anything was heading in our direction you'd be hearing all kinds of alarms and–'

27

Everyone jumped.

'What's that?' said Tori.

'An alarm, as it happens,' said Doctor Planetnoggin. 'Let me see what's going on.' He studied his computer monitor. 'Ah. It appears this is a previously undiscovered asteroid and its course will in fact bring it somewhat close to Earth. That's totally, totally fun! I shouldn't worry, though, kids. My colleague Doctor Paxton is an expert on asteroids and if this one were on a collision course with us he'd be in here screaming and shouting about it, so there's really no need to—'

The door flew open and a tall, thin man exploded into the room, waving his arms about madly. 'Waaaaaaaah!' he yelled before

28

colliding with a filing cabinet and collapsing in a heap. A plant pot toppled off, struck him on the head and shattered, leaving a clump of soil and a plant sprouting out of the top of his head.

'Doctor Paxton?' said Doctor Planetnoggin. 'What's going on? Explain yourself, dude. We're in the middle of some serious funstronomy here!'

'The asteroid's going to hit us! We're done for!' cried the tall, thin man.

The children gasped. Someone let out a scream. Tori grabbed Lance's hand.

'What?' said Mr Taylor. 'You can't be serious? Are you actually claiming that an asteroid is going to collide with the Earth?'

'No doubt about it,' replied Doctor Paxton. He clawed the soil and the plant off his head.

29

'I just worked it out. We've got until Friday – four days. That's all. Just four days until the asteroid hits and wipes out all life on the planet. No doubt, no mistake. It's definitely going to happen. This really is it, everyone. It's the end of the world!'

There was a very, very, very long silence.

'Whoa,' said Doctor Planetnoggin at last. 'That's totally, totally not fun.'

Peach raised her hand. 'Can we have some ice cream now, sir?'

CHAPTER TWO
DEATH BY PEACH

The news that the world was going to end on Friday seriously miffed a lot of people, particularly those with plans for the weekend. Angry letters were written to newspapers; irate calls were made to radio phone-ins and over a hundred and twenty-five thousand signatures were collected for a petition before it was realised that petitions were

powerless to stop enormous lumps of rock from slamming into the Earth.

Representatives of all the world's nations assembled hastily with the goal of finding some solution to the asteroid problem. But before their discussions could begin, an argument broke out about the seating plan in the meeting hall. The representative from the UK wanted to sit next to the representative from the USA, but found the representative from Ireland had already taken that seat. The UK claimed it always sat next to the USA and, as one of its closest allies, should be allowed to sit there now. Ireland claimed it usually sat next to the USA. Furthermore, it claimed it was an even bigger ally of the USA than the UK, and anyway it was first come first served. The UK stamped

its foot and said that wasn't fair. In a bid to calm the situation, the USA suggested the UK sit next to Mexico, which was nearby. The UK shook its head fiercely and said that just wasn't the same. Then Ireland stuck out its tongue at the UK. The UK's bottom lip wobbled and it stormed off, choking back tears and declaring that it was going to sit next to Denmark, which was better than the silly old USA and Ireland put together, and Denmark had biscuits too. But then Norway claimed it always sat next to Denmark. By the time the seating arrangements had been agreed to everyone's satisfaction, it was time for lunch, and a whole new argument broke out about how many sausages you were allowed to take from the buffet. At about three o'clock that afternoon it was decided

33

to postpone discussion of the asteroid until the next day, so that everyone would have had a good night's sleep, and all the nations of the world were expected to be a good deal less grumpy and naughty.

Meanwhile, the world's scientists had been busily contacting one another via a social networking website called Cleverweb, firstly to confirm the existence of the asteroid and its deadly trajectory, and secondly to try to figure out how to stop it from hitting Earth.

One scientist named Doctor Killian Crunch announced that there was no need to panic. He had made it his life's work to prepare for the possibility of such a rogue asteroid and had developed a sure-fire plan to deflect it. Upon inspection, however, this sure-fire plan appeared to involve launching huge amounts of lettuce

34

into low-Earth orbit, an action that the doctor claimed would create an impenetrable lettuce-barrier and cause the asteroid to bounce harmlessly away from Earth. Doctor Crunch then let it be known that he owned the second-largest lettuce farm in Europe and could provide the required amount of the vegetable for a mere twenty-four billion pounds.

The world's scientists issued a collective sigh and de-friended him on Cleverweb.

There was talk among many of firing a nuclear missile into space to destroy the asteroid. But when the scientists suggested this, the world's military leaders had sheepishly to admit that no one actually had nuclear weapons any more. They had all been dismantled years ago because it had been thought much simpler and cheaper

just to let people think they still existed.

At this point the world's scientists gave up and started playing computer games instead.

Computer keys clicked like chattering teeth. Encyclopaedia pages swished like the wind.

'Hello,' said a pleasant voice from the TV screen in the corner of the room. 'We hope you're having a lovely Tuesday afternoon. This is *Asteroid Watch,* your number one source of information about the end of the world. Stay with us because coming up later in the show we've got some super recipes you can make with any leftovers you may have about the house after the recent food riots, a guide to all the best shops to loot in your area, plus of course all the very latest news about Asteroid Peach

and the coming apocalypse itself.'

'Asteroid Peach!' muttered Lance. 'That is so unfair on so many different levels.'

'I hardly think the name of the thing is our main problem, is it?' said Tori.

The living room door opened. 'You two kids all right?' said Mrs Spratley. 'Need a cuppa? Although, I'm afraid we've no milk.' She paused. 'Or tea, actually. So it'll be just hot water . . . well, I say hot. The kettle's broken and Sally's just used the last of the hot water from the immersion to wash her doll's hair. So it'll just be cold tap water, I'm afraid . . . well, rainwater actually. The taps have packed up and there's no one to fix them. So, what do you say? A nice cup of cold rainwater each, mmm?'

'Maybe later, Mum,' said Lance, not looking up from the pages of his encyclopaedia.

'We're still trying to find a way to stop the asteroid. There must be some bit of information the authorities are overlooking.' He stopped and looked up excitedly. 'Imagine if we did, Mum! If the world was saved by us, the Knowledge Warriors.'

'Knowledge Champions,' said Tori, continuing to tap away on her laptop.

'Yeah, right,' muttered Lance.

'Still watching that silly programme?' asked Mrs Spratley, nodding at the television which was now burbling away to itself about what certain celebrities were going to wear at one of the many fashionable end-of-world parties being held on Friday.

Lance nodded. 'It keeps us up to date with the latest on the asteroid – in between all the silly stuff.'

'This asteroid business is a lot of fuss about nothing, I'm sure,' said Mrs Spratley. 'These things usually are. Mark my words. If you want me I'll be in the kitchen having a cup of tea. Well, I say tea. . .' She closed the door behind her.

Lance smiled weakly. 'Sorry about Mum,' he said to Tori. 'I think she lost a few I.Q. points after that being-transformed-into-

40

jelly business last year. She makes great pancakes now, though.'

Tori nodded. 'My Aunt Hazel's just as clueless about the asteroid and she doesn't even have the excuse of being re-materialised. I just think some things are just too big for people to grasp.'

Lance threw down his encyclopaedia. 'Oh, this is pointless!' he sighed. 'If the world's greatest scientists can't figure out a way to stop the asteroid, why should we be able to?'

'We saved the world once before,' said Tori firmly. 'We can do it again.'

Lance snorted. 'What were we up against then? One measly space lizard and his pet dinosaur. But this is different. You can't outwit an asteroid any more than a person falling off a ladder can outwit the ground.'

He laughed bitterly.

'There's always something you can do,' said Tori.

'But what if there isn't?' said Lance. 'What if this is what's supposed to happen? An asteroid hit the Earth sixty-five million years ago and wiped out the dinosaurs. But then the mammals filled the gap they left in the environment and here we are today. Maybe the human race is supposed to be destroyed on Friday afternoon so some other species can have a go at ruling the Earth.' He let out a huge sigh.

'Blimey,' said Tori. 'You're a right flipping bundle of laughs, aren't you?'

The telephone rang. Lance picked up the receiver. 'Hello?'

'Lance!' said a familiar voice. 'Hello, mate.

42

PC Sledge here.'

'Hi there,' said Lance. 'I bet your little house guest is loving this, isn't he? We go to all the bother of saving the world and now it's going to be destroyed by a bit of old rock. He must be laughing his little scaly socks off.'

'Funny you should say that,' said PC Sledge. 'Because that's actually why I'm calling. Admiral Skink reckons he knows how to stop Asteroid Peach hitting the planet. He's actually offering to help.'

CHAPTER THREE
A SPACE LIZARD IN DOWNING STREET

The black limousine glided along Whitehall. Inside, perched forward on its plush leather seats, were Lance Spratley, his parents, his sister Sally and his best friend Tori Walnut. All were dry-mouthed and butterfly-tummied at the prospect of what was about to happen. All except Sally, that is, who was just excited to be out of the house, and was showing this

by kicking Lance repeatedly in the shins.

The street bustled with people. At first, the announcement of the impending arrival of Asteroid Peach had disrupted the normal patterns of life: widespread rioting and looting had broken out across the world and schools and places of work had closed to allow people to spend the last few days of planet Earth with their families. But, after a day of being cooped up with their relatives, watching the expensive TVs they had pinched from nearby electrical shops, most people found themselves going crazy with boredom and had gone back to their daily routines as quickly as possible.

The limo slowed to a halt in front of the tall iron gates at the entrance to Downing Street. A policeman approached and spoke to the

driver, then made a tick on a clipboard. The gates swung open and the limo slithered inside.

'Imagine us meeting the Prime Minister!' said Mrs Spratley and giggled with delight. 'Who'd have thought it? I wish I'd voted for him now. Or for anyone, really. I really should take more interest in world affairs, what with the world ending and everything.'

Lance smiled to himself. His parents' radical personality changes following their molecular reassembly from blue wobbling jellies still surprised him. They were so much more cheerful and easy-going – if ever so slightly less bright – than they were before. Lance loved his new parents but also expected that he would eventually miss the old ones who used to boss him about.

Although so far he hadn't missed them a bit.

'Don't kick your brother, there's good girl, eh?' said Mr Spratley to Sally with a patient smile. Sally sighed and let her legs flop limply, a look of tremendous boredom on her face. She cheered herself up by blowing raspberries instead.

Sally's molecules had also been rearranged by Admiral Skink's energy weapon, but Lance found her so hard to fathom most of the time that he couldn't tell whether her personality had been affected or not. As far as he could tell, she didn't so much have a personality, more a collection of annoying habits, all of which seemed exactly the same as before.

She could be entertaining, though. Last week she had practically destroyed the family computer by trying to feed a frozen

47

mini-pizza into its CD drive. It made Lance giggle just to think about it.

The limo drew to a halt outside the familiar black front door of Number Ten. There was a click from within and the door swung open.

The Prime Minister adjusted his glasses and ran his eyes over the file marked *The Cottleton Incident*. It had been prepared for him a couple of months ago by the Secret Service. He had meant to read it at the time but been distracted by a cupcake and forgotten all about it. He adjusted his glasses and skimmed the pages hurriedly. *Dinosaur . . . rampage . . . space lizard . . . two schoolchildren . . .* Ah yes. He remembered one of his advisers mentioning it now. Despite the sensational subject matter, The Cottleton Incident wasn't

a subject that interested him terribly because there didn't appear to be anything in it for which he could take personal credit, and what the Prime Minister loved to do more than almost anything was take credit for things. He closed the file and placed it on his desk. 'This space lizard chappie is on his way here now, is he?' he asked his Defence Secretary.

'Yes, Prime Minister,' said the Defence Secretary. 'Along with the two schoolchildren who defeated him. We invited their families too as a bit of PR. Except the girl has no family. Other than an aunt. And she couldn't come because she has to look after some poorly rabbits or something . . . '

'All right. No need to give me their entire life stories. What's your assessment of the situation?'

49

'Well, PM,' began the Defence Secretary. 'If we can help the lizard prevent the asteroid strike, it saves the world and that'll do absolute wonders for your popularity. If we can't and the world ends – well, the world's ended hasn't it, so no one's around to notice that your plan didn't work.'

The Prime Minister nodded. 'Yes, those

are my feelings, too. Very much a win-win situation.'

'Except,' said the Defence Secretary, 'I wouldn't really call the end of the world a "win", exactly.'

'No, I suppose not. Got any cupcakes on you?' replied the Prime Minister, who was already a little bit bored of the whole end-of- the-world problem.

'Erm, no, Prime Minister. Shall I order your Private Secretary to send out for some?'

'Excellent idea!'

'At once, sir.' The Defence Secretary nodded and slunk from the office.

The intercom on the Prime Minister's desk buzzed.

'The visitors are here, sir,' said a voice.

A member of Downing Street staff led Tori and the Spratleys into the office. Lance's heart leaped when he saw the Prime Minister himself – the Right Honourable Mr Jarvis Pocket, MP, complete with his famous floppy fringe and glasses, sitting behind a vast oak desk. The staff member showed them to a row of luxurious leather seats and they sat, palms sweating and tummies icy with anticipation. The office was large and filled with antique furniture. From its dark, oak-panelled walls, imposing portraits of previous Prime Ministers stared down at them with stern eyes.

Behind his desk, the Prime Minister marshalled the muscles of his face into a smile. After two years in the job, he had almost perfected the art of smiling at will.

For smiling did not come easily to him, at least, not smiling at insignificant commoners like those now seated before him. He was able to smile easily at big piles of money, or at winning an election, or at his favourite thing in the entire world – cupcakes. But faced with ordinary people and their worthless petty problems and awful cheap clothes, he had to work hard simply to prevent his expression from shrivelling into one of utter disgust – and that is never an appealing look for a politician. Producing a workable smile that could be shown in public had taken months of gruelling exercise and coaching from some of the country's top media gurus. It was a struggle but now, at last, he could manage it if he tried.

'Hello there,' he said in as friendly a manner

as he was able. He relaxed his facial muscles. No point in overstraining them – he might need them later. He cast his gaze at Lance and Tori. 'I take it you are the brave pair who saved the town of Cottington from the space lizard?'

'Cottleton, actually,' said Tori.

'And it wasn't just our town we saved. It was the whole world,' corrected Lance.

'That's what I like to hear,' said the Prime Minister in a cheery voice. 'Young people aiming high! Splendid!'

Lance and Tori exchanged a confused look.

'Anyway,' said the Prime Minister, 'to business. As I'm sure you are aware, we're in a bit of a pickle with this asteroid. There's nothing anyone can do to prevent it hitting us – or so we thought. Now your space lizard

is claiming he can save the day. Whether he can or not remains to be seen. But as you have had dealings with him in the past it seemed wise to ask you here today to hear what he has to say. Do you think we can trust him?'

Lance spluttered. 'Trust him? The creature who tried to conquer our planet? Are you completely mad?'

The eyes of the Prime Minister widened.

'Lance!' hissed Mrs Spratley out of the side of her mouth. 'Don't question the Prime Minister's sanity! It's not polite!' She gave a genteel laugh. 'What I think my son is trying to say—'

'Lance's right,' interrupted Tori. 'Admiral Skink is a maniac. There's no way on Earth anyone should trust a word that comes out of his scaly little cakehole.'

The Prime Minister nodded slowly and made his fingers into a steeple, which is something he did when he hadn't the faintest idea what to say but wanted to appear wise. What if this space lizard made outrageous demands in return for helping? What if he asked for the Crown Jewels? Or land? What if wanted his own kingdom? How much of the UK could the Prime Minister conceivably give away to an alien creature without losing too much popularity? *Scotland,* he thought suddenly. *I could let him have Scotland. No one from there has ever liked me.* But what if Admiral Skink wanted even more than that? He heaved a sigh and wished at that moment that he was a thousand miles away listening to a rugby match on the radio and opening a box of cupcakes – chocolate ones,

preferably, with chocolate cream interiors and sparkly vanilla frosting . . .

The intercom on his desk buzzed. 'Admiral Skink has arrived,' said a voice.

A sudden chill gripped the room. Tori felt all the hairs on the back of her neck stand on end.

'I see,' said the Prime Minister, stirring from his daydream. 'I suppose you'd better show him in, then.'

'Just remember,' said Lance, 'whatever he says, whatever he wants or claims he can do to help – don't trust him.'

'Thank you for your input, children,' said the Prime Minister.

There was a sudden sound of trumpets, a stirring fanfare. The door opened and into the room came the broad, uniformed

shape of PC Sledge. He was carrying before him with slow solemnity a large cushion made of red velvet. Reclining on the cushion and wearing an expression of extreme lizardly delight and self-importance sat the iguana formerly known as Pickles – the body within which lurked the mind of the Grand Leader of the Swerdlixian Lizard Swarm himself, Admiral Skink. Lance noticed that the music was coming from a portable CD player slung on a strap over PC Sledge's shoulder. The fanfare reached a triumphant crescendo. The human occupants of the room stared in bemusement at the plump green form sprawling on the cushion. The iguana's thin green lips parted and it flashed a sickly reptilian smile with its sharp triangular teeth.

'Sorry about this,' said PC Sledge, his face reddening. 'But he insisted. Said he wouldn't help unless we started treating him with a bit more respect.'

'Silence, mammal!' croaked Admiral Skink in his scratchy voice. 'Your superior is waiting to speak.' He flashed his small, cold eyes at the figure seated behind the oak desk. 'Ah. Good afternoon, Prime Minister.'

The Prime Minister's eyebrows danced

a jig of astonishment. 'H-h-hello . . . ' he stammered. A shiver passed through him and he had the sudden feeling of being in the unmistakable presence of pure evil. He had experienced this only once before in his life, when an older boy at his public school had stolen his football boots and covered them in gravy. The boy's mocking laughter still haunted his dreams. He shook himself. 'Good afternoon, Admiral,' he said, his confidence returning. 'I believe you have a proposition to put to us?'

Admiral Skink chuckled. 'Indeed I do. An asteroid is three days away from hitting this world and extinguishing your feeble little . . . ah excuse me, your wonderful civilisation. Sadly, you ape creatures are powerless to save yourselves. The technology required is far beyond your grasp. It is not, however,

beyond mine.' He paused dramatically. Somewhere in the room an old grandfather clock ticked loudly.

'So . . . ?' said the Prime Minister hopefully.

'So,' said Admiral Skink, 'under my command you shall build a device known as an omega wave projector. Don't ask how it works because your human minds could not begin to understand it. With this device we shall project an omega wave into space and shatter the asteroid into harmless space dust.'

'Why should we trust you?' asked the Prime Minister.

'Because, sir, I am your only hope of salvation,' said Admiral Skink.

'But what do you want in return?' asked Lance.

'Yeah,' added Tori. 'I bet you're not doing this out of the kindness of your heart.'

She gave the lizard a hard stare.

'A fair question,' said the Prime Minister.

Admiral Skink muttered something to PC Sledge and the policeman turned on his heel so that the iguana was now facing the other visitors. 'Why hello, children!' said Admiral Skink in a friendly voice. 'How delightful to see you again.' He grinned and waved a long-toed claw at Lance and Tori.

The two children stared back, meeting his gaze without fear.

'You don't fool us for one second!' hissed Tori. 'I might have fallen for your fairy tales last time, but if you think I'm going to let you bamboozle us again you've made a big mistake, buster!'

Impressed, and ever-so-slightly scared by this furious outburst from Tori, Lance nodded

in agreement. 'That's right,' he added in as tough a voice as he could manage, which wasn't really very tough at all.

'So what do you want, Admiral?' asked the Prime Minister, crossing his fingers under his desk and silently wishing to himself *Please don't say the Crown Jewels, please don't say the Crown Jewels* . . .

'Oh, I don't ask for much,' said Admiral Slink. 'I appreciate the fact that I am a prisoner on this world and must remain so. All I want is to be moved to a larger vivarium. One with a view of the outside world. It would be nice to see the sunset sometimes while I am munching a Scramthorn leaf. That is all.'

The Prime Minister leaped to his feet and thrust out his hand. 'I do believe we have a deal!' he said.

PC Sledge turned and shuffled towards the Prime Minister's desk. Admiral Skink extended a claw and shook the Prime Minister's hand. 'Thank you,' he said quietly. 'I shall do my best for your world.'

'Oh brilliant!' said Lance, rolling his eyes. 'That's humanity knackered, then.'

'Thank you for coming, children,' said the Prime Minister curtly. 'You've been a great help.'

'But you have to realise–!' began Tori.

'I said thank you,' said the Prime Minister firmly. 'That will be all.' He looked with gratitude at the scaly green creature curled up on the red cushion and felt the muscles of his face form themselves spontaneously into the biggest smile he had managed all year.

CHAPTER FOUR
OMEGA WAVE GOODBYE

Music blared – an urgent parping that seemed to grab you by your lapels and shake you until you gave it your complete attention. From behind a desk the size of a swimming pool, a beautiful face topped by an elaborate bouffant of sculpted blonde hair opened its mouth, revealing a set of gorgeous, snow-white – and outrageously expensive – teeth.

The mouth spoke:

'Hello America! You're watching the Weasel Corporation News Network. It's nine o'clock and I'm Ophelia Krudd. Here are the top stories in the world today, sponsored by Sparklefresh Flamethrowers, the zingingest flamethrowers around. Hollywood heart-throb Zip Barstow denies his marriage to rap diva Fayetta Spume is a publicity stunt to promote his latest range of mayonnaise. In New York City, a cypress tree has been voted mayor after all the human candidates in the election dropped out due to scandals. This makes the third tree to gain elected office in the USA this month. Asteroid fever hits Sacramento, California, where people have gone wild over the delicious asteroid-shaped cookies being sold by Girl Scouts to raise

money for an asteroid shelter to protect the city's inhabitants. So far the ingenious gals have raised nearly a thousand dollars. Scientists say the shelter will be useless. And finally – over in London, England, work is completed on the so-called 'omega wave projector' which the British Prime Minister is claiming will destroy Asteroid Peach and save the planet Earth from an impending fiery doom. For more on that last story, here's our reporter Franklin Podd, who is standing beside a large photograph of 10 Downing Street right now.'

An eerily handsome man, whom you would have sworn was a tailor's dummy somehow magically brought to life, fixed the viewers at home with a stern – yet reassuring – stare and clasped his microphone tightly.

67

'Thanks, Ophelia! A statement from 10 Downing Street this morning said that the device is ready to operate and will be switched on at three p.m. local time, that's ten a.m. Eastern Standard Time. I'll guess then we'll find out whether the estimated six hundred and seventy-six trillion pounds the device cost to manufacture was worth it.'

'Pretty pricey, huh? How does it work, Franklin?'

'Good question, Ophelia! No one seems to know. There's been a blanket of secrecy over this whole shebang. None of the scientists or component manufacturers working on the project has been allowed to speak to the press. However, there are numerous rumours circulating about the omega wave projector and Asteroid Peach itself. Some people are

claiming that the omega wave projector will not destroy Asteroid Peach at all but will instead slow it down to a point where it will land gently on the Earth, merely crushing the place it lands on rather than devastating the entire planet. Most people seem to think that place will be the city of Warrington – home of the North Cheshire Wind Orchestra – in northern England and that its destruction will be a small price to pay for saving the world. Another theory has it that there is no Asteroid Peach and that this whole end-of-the-world thing is a hoax dreamed up by the British to help their ailing economy. A recent survey found that eighty per cent of the American public believe that Asteroid Peach does not exist.'

'But what about all the scientific evidence

for the asteroid's existence, Franklin? How can people ignore that?'

'I think the most popular method is closing your eyes and sticking your fingers in your ears whenever a scientist appears on television. Another source swears blind that the omega wave projector is the idea of – get this – an alien lizard creature whose mind is trapped inside the body of a common iguana. This "space lizard", if you will, is some kind of galactic criminal or warlord and is promising to save the planet in return for some kind of lessening of his prison sentence. Kooky stuff, Ophelia, which, needless to say, I think we can safely discount!'

'A space lizard, you say? I've heard some crazy nonsense in my time, Franklin, but that one takes the cake! Thanks for your report.

Now we go live to New York where the new mayor is about to be officially replanted in City Hall park. . . '

Meanwhile in London, Hyde Park was a sea of excited chatter, bobbing with rock festival amounts of smiling heads and flashing cameras. The heads and cameras were all pointing towards a hastily assembled stage standing in the centre of a wide expanse of grass. The stage had originally been built that morning in Downing Street, but after stupendous quantities of people had clogged the streets around Whitehall, desperate for a glimpse of the wondrous machine that would save the world, the Prime Minister had ordered it moved to Hyde Park to accommodate the ever-swelling crowd of onlookers.

In the middle of the stage sat a most extraordinary-looking object. It was an enormous transparent sphere, over thirty metres in diameter, its surface featureless and perfectly smooth. The sphere glinted brilliantly in the sunlight like a soap bubble blown by some giant child. To one side of the immense sphere were ranged a few rows of seats for dignitaries, at which sat several politicians, pop stars, a bishop or two, and Lance, Tori and the other Spratleys. To the other side stood a gaggle of white-coated scientists, each of them wearing an expression of anxious anticipation. With them was PC Sledge, and with him, perched regally on his red velvet cushion, was Admiral Skink, his tiny triangular teeth flashing in a grin of smug satisfaction and pride. In front

of the sphere stood a lectern on which could be seen a microphone and a laptop computer. Behind the lectern, tapping the microphone with his finger to make sure it was working, was the Prime Minister, his floppy fringe flapping in the breeze. He shot a glance at one of the white-coated scientists. The scientist returned a thumbs-up sign. The Prime Minister cleared his throat.

'Ladies and gentlemen,' his amplified voice boomed around the park, silencing the crowd in an instant, 'today is an auspicious day for the human race. We stand poised on the brink of utter annihilation. The life of every one of us is in mortal danger, and every achievement gained throughout the history of our species – be it technological, cultural, political or philosophical – hangs by a thread

73

over an abyss of total destruction.'

'Get on with it!' shouted a voice from the crowd. It sounded to Lance very much like the girl Jasmine from his class at school. Another voice giggled. Peach, Lance was sure.

'I'm bored,' muttered Sally, kicking the legs of her chair. 'Hasn't the world ended yet?' A few of the bishops and other dignitaries sitting around them made harrumphing noises. This was supposed to be a solemn, dignified occasion. Lance shushed his sister, covering his mouth with his hand to hide his smirk.

The Prime Minister frowned with annoyance. He consulted his notes on the lectern. 'Where was I? Ah yes. Total destruction. The final days of the planet Earth and all the life it holds may be at hand. Or – thanks to this

marvellous device you see behind me, thanks to the superb work of some of Britain's most talented scientists and technicians, thanks to the resourcefulness of the human race, and of course thanks to me for bringing them all together – we may yet have a chance!'

A tremendous roar erupted from the crowd. Hats were tossed into the air and then politely passed back to their owners.

The Prime Minister heaved the muscles of his face into a smile. He really was getting quite good at that now.

'This device is called an omega wave projector. It will transmit its rays into space and excite the molecules of Asteroid Peach until it shatters into harmless fragments, saving our world!'

Once again, the crowd went bananas.

The Prime Minister raised his hands to quieten them.

'The time for talk is over. Now, at last, is the time for action. So without further ado, it gives me immense pride and pleasure to officially switch on this fantastic British-made omega wave projector – which was my idea!'

The noise from the crowd was deafening.

He raised a single finger theatrically and brought it down on to one of the laptop's keys. . .

The crowd fell silent. . .

Lance and Tori craned their necks forward to get a better view. . .

The laptop emitted a beep. . .

The giant transparent sphere of the omega wave projector . . . failed to do anything.

77

After a few seconds . . . it continued not to do anything.

Lance and Tori exchanged frowns.

The Prime Minister's smile began to slide off his face. He pressed the button on the laptop again.

Then again.

And still the omega wave projector just sat there, steadfastly refusing to work.

He looked at the white-coated scientist. The scientist shrugged and then looked down at his feet.

For a long, long time there was silence, save for the quiet thump-thump-thump of Sally's shoes clattering against her chair.

Somewhere in the distance, a crow cawed with delight at finding a worm. Sadly, this had no effect on the omega wave projector.

78

Now that the smile had vacated the Prime Minister's face, a look of panic moved in and made itself very much at home.

The crowd began to emit a few confused grunts. The Prime Minister gulped. He knew those noises well. You do not become Prime Minister without understanding the behaviour of crowds. He knew that in a few short moments the confused grunting would stop, and the terrifying howls of rage and calls for his blood would begin. He looked around, searching for an exit – and was astonished to see Admiral Skink spring down from his cushion and bound over towards him. Ignoring the Prime Minister, the little iguana scampered up the lectern and took hold of the microphone in one of his scaly, long-toed claws.

'Inhabitants of Planet Earth!' boomed Admiral Skink in an amused voice. 'Listen to me and listen well!'

A strange silence fell across the crowd.

'What now?' wondered a stray voice. 'A puppet show?'

'I have,' continued Admiral Skink, 'in my capacity as Grand Ruler of the Swerdlixian Lizard Swarm, encountered many, many species of low intelligence on my travels in the galaxy, including the Tiny-Brained Maggotworms of Dimm XV and the Mindless Rock Ponies of the Granite Meadows of Klakk. But you lot – the human race of the planet Earth – are, I have to say, without doubt the thickest of the whole bunch! Your own British Prime Minister, in particular, is a spectacular example of your species' stupidity. This device I have made you

assemble is not an omega wave projector! There is no such thing as an omega wave projector, you ignorant monkeys! This device is a wormhole bridge! It opens a rip in the fabric of space/time from here to a point of my own choosing, that point being, of course, my home planet of Swerdlix! Perhaps I shall train a telescope on this world from my own so that in a few years' time, when the light has reached me, I shall see Asteroid Peach smash into you and wipe you all out – and when that moment comes, humans, I will giggle. Ta-ta!'

Admiral Skink tapped a few keys on the laptop. A door suddenly appeared in the side of the great transparent sphere and slid open with a pleasing hum. Admiral Skink bounded down from the lectern, his long tail bobbing with glee, and went through the door into

81

the sphere. He turned and winked at the crowd. There was a sudden fizzing, crackling sound and a burst of brilliant blue light. When the light died away a fraction of a second later, Admiral Skink had vanished.

The crowd started doing the confused grunting thing again.

The Prime Minister's face went red, then white, then blue in a patriotic display of extreme discomfort. He clutched at his chest. His heart seemed to be trying to make up its mind whether to stop, explode or melt like an ice-lolly in the sun. There was a cupcake in the glove compartment of his car. He wished he had brought it with him.

Lance was shaking his head. 'I knew it,' he muttered. 'I knew Skink would find some way to cheat us.'

Tori touched his hand. 'There's still time. We'll think of something. You'll see.'

Lance looked into a sky and saw a bright speck of light, like a silvery crumb suspended in the air. Asteroid Peach was now visible with the naked eye.

'At least things can't get any worse.' Tori continued.

Then, to make matters worse, a giant, long-necked lizard-creature with jaws the size of sofas suddenly materialised within the sphere that Admiral Skink had just disappeared through. It squeezed out through the door, its brilliant purple scales glistening in the afternoon sunlight, sniffed the air a couple of times, and then ate Sally Spratley.

CHAPTER FIVE
REAL BRAINS

'OWWWWW! OWWW! OWWWWWWWWWWWWW!'

It could have been worse, the Prime Minister reflected a little later. It could have been much worse.

'OWWWWW!!! OW! OWWWWWW!'

At least the giant purple lizard-creature had frightened away most of the angry crowd. Faced with the sudden appearance

84

of a hideous alien monster, the majority of the assembled masses had lost their desire to take out their frustrations at the failure of the omega wave projector on the Prime Minister, and scarpered niftily out of Hyde Park. Those that remained looked too shocked to do anything.

'OW! OW! OW! OWWWWWWWWWWWWWWW!!!'

Which left the Prime Minister with just two small problems. Firstly, the world was still going to be destroyed in a couple of days' time. And secondly, he himself was almost certainly going to be destroyed much sooner by the family of the young girl whom the giant purple lizard-creature had just swallowed.

'Owwwww!' shrieked the Prime Minister. 'Mrs Spratley! Please let go of my hair!' He looked around for his bodyguards and saw

85

them slumped against the stage playing Guess Who? One of them looked in his direction briefly and then lowered his eyes to the game once more. The Prime Minister began to suspect they were not impressed at the failure of the omega wave projector, either.

'My poor little daughter's in that thing!' cried Mrs Spratley, pointing at the giant purple lizard-creature, which was now lazing contentedly on the stage. Lance, Tori and Mr Spratley were all thumping and kicking the creature in a frantic bid to make it spit Sally out, but the creature seemed barely aware of the pummelling it was receiving. 'My little Sally! What are you going to do about it?'

'Mrs Spratley, I assure you that I would be delighted to personally arrange compensation

of a most generous– **OWWWWWWWWWWW!**
Stop it, please!'

'Compensation?' bellowed Mrs Spratley.
'I don't think so! What I want is my daughter
and I want her NOW! Got it?' She gave the
Prime Minister's fringe a final savage tug and
he sank to his knees in a snivelling heap.

It sounded to Lance like his mother was
becoming her old self.

'Hold up,' said a voice. 'What this situation
requires is real brains.'

Lance and the others looked round and saw
PC Sledge hurrying towards them.

'Great – do you know someone with real
brains who can help us?' asked Lance.

PC Sledge gave him a glare.

'Oh, I see,' said Lance. 'Sorry.'

The policeman stroked his chin and looked

the great purple reptile up and down. 'This here is a type of Thrall-Beast,' he said.

'Thrall-Beast?' asked Lance.

'It's a type of servant lizard on Admiral Skink's home planet, isn't it?' said Tori. 'I remember him telling me that when he was using Lance's body.'

'That's right,' PC Sledge replied, sounding ever so slightly smug. 'And I have these last few months become something of an expert on Admiral Skink's home planet and its ways. Old Skinky talked about nothing else when he was locked up at my station. Well, that and how much he missed eating something called a sparkworm. Yes, what I reckon we have here is a trash-eating Thrall-Beast used for cleaning the streets of the Swerdlixian Lizards' capital city.'

'Fascinating, I'm sure,' said Mrs Spratley. 'But how does that help us?'

'These beasties have extremely slow metabolisms,' said PC Sledge. 'I reckon young Sally will be fine in there.' He pressed his ear against the monster's long neck. 'Ah yes. Just as I thought.'

'What do you mean?' asked Mrs Spratley.

'Have a listen for yourself,' said PC Sledge.

The remaining Spratley family and Tori all pressed their heads against the neck of the lizard-creature.

'Hello?' called a muffled but familiar voice from within.

'Sally!' cried Mrs Spratley. 'You're alive!'

'Are you all right?' asked Lance.

'No!' called Sally's voice. 'I'm really, really, really bored! There's nothing to do in here at all!

It's almost as bad as Auntie Chrissy's house.'

'We'll get you out of there as soon as possible, I promise,' said Lance. 'Either that or we'll send in a good book and a torch.'

'From what the Admiral tells me it seems these creatures are always eating stuff they're not supposed to, back on Swerdlix,' said PC Sledge. 'What the lizards do is make the creatures sneeze and the stuff stuck in their throats shoots straight out.'

'And how, may I ask, do you make one of these monsters sneeze?' asked Mrs Spratley, gazing at the great scaly beast. 'Got an industrial-sized sack of sneezing powder in the back of your car, have you?'

'It's simple,' said PC Sledge. 'According to the Admiral all you have to do is sprinkle flooblescoop powder in its nostrils.'

'Flooble-what?'

'Flooblescoop powder. A specific chemical substance derived from the bark of the flooblescoop shrub, a plant species native to the planet Swerdlix.'

'And how are we supposed to get this powder if it's native only to Admiral Skink's planet?' asked Mrs Spratley.

PC Sledge thought about this for a moment and then his face fell. 'Ah. I suspect you may

have spotted a flaw in my plan.'

'Real brains indeed!' said Mrs Spratley. 'And what about you lot?' she called to a gaggle of white-coated scientists who were huddled around the laptop on the lectern trying to find out how to reopen the vortex. Although so far they'd been unsuccessful because of Admiral Skink's encryptions. 'Can any of you eggheads help get my daughter out of this beast?' Mrs Spratley continued.

The scientists came over to the creature and began prodding it and making little noises of curiosity. One of them took out a ruler and began making measurements, more out of habit than anything else. The creature ignored them.

Lance looked over at the lectern, frowning. An idea was beginning to form slowly in his

mind, like the way an icicle is formed by the steady drip-drip-drip of water. It felt like it was going to be a good one.

He took Tori by the sleeve and led her to the lectern. He began to tap the keys of the laptop.

'Aha! Just as I suspected!'

'What are you doing?' said Tori. 'The controls are encrypted, aren't they?'

'They sure are,' said Lance. 'Admiral Skink is a genius compared to most Earth people. If he wanted to, he could have placed security measures on this system that no one would be able to crack in a thousand years.'

'If he wanted to? You mean he didn't?'

'It appears not,' replied Lance. His fingers flitted over the keys. 'In fact it looks like all he did was protect the machine's controls with

a single password. He might be an evil genius, but he's a dead lazy one.'

'A password? Can we guess it?'

Lance smiled. 'I already have.' He pressed a final key.

Tori's eyes widened to the size of Wagon Wheels. She let out an excited giggle.

Next to the laptop lay a pile of papers – the Prime Minister's speech, and sitting next to that was an expensive gold-plated fountain pen, presumably the Prime Minister's too. Lance took the pen and hastily scribbled the words: *Gone through wormhole. Will try to save world and find some Flooblescoop powder to rescue Sally too. Back soon! Lance & Tori* on the back of one of the sheets of paper.

Unnoticed by the others, they tiptoed over to the great transparent sphere where even

now a small door was forming in its dazzling surface. They went inside.

'So what was the password?' asked Tori.

'His favourite thing, of course,' said Lance, smiling. 'His favourite type of snack, to be precise – sparkworms!'

There was a brilliant flash of blue light and then they were gone.

CHAPTER SIX
SLANGFASH REVISITED

One thousand one hundred and one light years away, on a hot and humid, dust-blasted planet orbiting a bloated, burgundy-coloured supergiant star, an iguana scurried along a wide, stony road in the centre of a bustling city, towards a glittering metallic palace.

The iguana's heart was filled with a delirious joy, for it had arrived at this place after a long

and painful absence. Its mind, on the other hand, was filled with hate, wickedness, petulance, anger, a sneering sense of superiority, and a great many other deeply unpleasant emotions, for the mind in question belonged, of course, to Admiral Skink.

The palace was a tall, conical structure. It resembled an enormous tooth that had pierced the skin of the planet from some savage higher dimension. It was blood red and dominated the buildings of the surrounding city like a giant preparing to stamp on them, a towering, brutish spike of a place.

It was also the place that Admiral Skink called home.

Around him, the Swerdlingham inhabitants went about their business. Strange insect-

97

like creatures sold energy vole kebabs and sky walrus burgers from rickety market stalls. Bright blue chicken-like birds raced this way and that on small, motorised skateboards, squawking madly. Thrall-Beasts of all sizes scuttled here and there on errands. And everywhere, with a cold, haughty pride, strolled members of the Swerdlixian Lizard Swarm themselves – ferocious-looking reptiles with cruel greeny-yellow eyes and long scaly tails. Admiral Skink recognised one or two of them, but dared not speak to them in his present form.

Near the entrance to Slangfash Palace, he hid behind a market stall and watched as a group of Swerdlixian Lizards waited to be admitted. The palace's huge metal mouth of a door slid open and the lizards trudged inside.

Admiral Skink scurried in with them, keeping himself low to the ground to avoid detection. Once inside the palace's wide, metallic lobby area, he knew he would be able to move freely as there were always numerous Thrall-Beasts about the palace carrying messages and takeaway snacks for the palace staff.

An air of dark foreboding clung to the palace's gleaming cylindrical form, as did a huge banner that read in the principal language of Swerdlix:

Admiral Skink blinked his tiny eyes in surprise. His scaly brow furrowed into a fierce frown. Then he noticed something else: a long, low building near the base of the palace. That was new.

'Check-in is this way, gentlemen,' said a familiar, rough voice.

Admiral Skink whirled around and saw a stocky female lizard with broad, beefy arms and a snarl on her large, doughy face. It was his niece Skinketta, he realised, one of his most trusted underlings. His spirits lifted to see her. Skinketta was the daughter of his brother, Captain Hornscrape. Hornscrape himself was weedy and ineffectual, but Skinketta was admirably brutal and loutish, if not exactly over-gifted with intelligence. But something was wrong. Skinketta wasn't

wearing her usual imperial war-jerkin and battle-pants as any self-respecting warrior lizard should. She was dressed, instead, in a ridiculous blue velvet outfit with a little cap and looked more like a shop assistant in some soppy boutique. What in the name of Kyross the Lizard God was going on?

After a short while, the group of lizards marched out of the lobby and trooped into a lift. There was a ping and the lift departed. Skinketta made a tick on a clipboard.

He would have to be quick. In his present iguana form, he could very easily wind up squashed flat under one of Skinketta's gigantic fists. This called for a mixture of speed and carefully judged nastiness.

Admiral Skink darted up to Skinketta and scampered with lightning speed up

her back and sat on top of her head. Then he wrapped his long tail around her neck, tightening his grip until Skinketta's eyes were bulging out like those of a shocked frog.

'Demented Thrall-Beast!' she bellowed, dropping her clipboard and clawing at her throat. 'How dare you attack your superior! You shall face a punishment of unimaginable agony for this–'

'Yeah, yeah,' interrupted Admiral Skink. 'Pipe down, Skinketta. It's me. Admiral Skink. Your Grand Ruler has returned.'

'Uncle?' whispered Skinketta in wonder. 'He who defeated the Faceless Atomic Hedgehogs of Joop and kicked the butts of the Splimrandian Combat Elks?'

'The very same,' hissed Admiral Skink.

'You've lost a bit of weight since the last time I saw you.'

'My mind is trapped in this Thrall-Beast's body, you brainless lump!' spat Admiral Skink. 'I used the Braintwizzler 360 Mind Migration System when my ship was destroyed and now I'm stuck in this body until I can be restored to my own.'

'But how do I know it's really you and not some imposter, O Lord?' gasped Skinketta.

'Because if you don't stop wasting my time I'm going to chop you up into little bits and sell you as a "Build Your Own Idiot" kit.'

'Ah!' cried Skinketta. 'That's what you said to me the last time we met! A hundred and ten thousand apologies, O Most Destructive Lizard Monarch! 'We had feared you lost forever! Admiral Gecko ordered us to –'

'Wait a minute! Admiral who?'

'Gecko, O Vanquisher of the Ganthorian Battle Mammoths. Our new Grand Ruler.'

'Your new WHAT?'

Skinketta felt Admiral Skink's tail tighten around her neck. 'He is our new Grand Ruler,' she croaked. 'He assumed command in a battle following the loss of your homing signal.'

'And is this Admiral Gecko responsible for turning my glittering palace into some cheap hotel and conference venue?'

'Indeed, O Indescribably Nasty Reptile King. He wants all the assets of the Swerdlixian Lizard Swarm to maximise their revenue streams and start earning their keep.'

Admiral Skink snorted. 'I go away for five minutes and this Gecko turns you all into accountants! Look at you in that ridiculous

104

get-up! This is no way for a Swerdlixian Lizard to behave! Where is your pride? Pah, there are going to be big changes around here. Mark my words.' He pointed at the elevator with his tail. 'Take me to my suite on the top floor. We will commence creation of a new body for me immediately from my private genetic codebank.'

'Begging your pardon, O Supreme Thug of the Cosmos, but Admiral Gecko has taken over your suite and turned it into an office for himself.'

Admiral Skink gasped. 'Then where are all my belongings? My spoils of war?'

Skinketta lowered her eyes. 'In the basement,' she said quietly. 'Awaiting disposal.'

Five minutes later, they had located most of the ex-Grand Ruler's belongings scattered along a dusty and disused corridor in the basement. Among them, they had retrieved the data file containing a readout of Admiral Skink's complete genetic code. Luckily, all senior Swerdlixian Lizards across the fleet had been required to keep such back-ups following the introduction of the Braintwizzler 360 Mind Migration Systems. Skinketta fed the information into an atomic reconfiguration unit that Admiral Skink had looted during a battle campaign against a neighbouring planet a few years previously.

The little iguana climbed inside the machine's huge glass tube.

'I am ready,' he called.

'Here we go, Uncle,' said Skinketta, flicking

a switch on the control panel.

A flickering green light filled the basement, illuminating a random assortment of weird skulls, obscure weapons, Scramthorn stalks and various other odds and ends Admiral Skink had picked up on his galactic travels.

'Commencing DNA re-sequence,' said Skinketta.

Light glimmered within the glass tube. Admiral Skink felt an odd tingling in his claws and tail, a sensation that rapidly spread to every part of his body. A raw electric power surged in his veins.

'Soon you will be reborn!' cried Skinketta. 'Soon you will revenge yourself on the betrayers of our civilisation! Soon the Swerdlixian Lizard Swarm will regain its rightful place as the supreme power in the universe!'

'All right,' said Admiral Skink. 'No need to make a big song and dance about it.'

Admiral Gecko sprawled in his enormous bingerscrawp-leather chair with his huge clawed feet up on his vast Wiffalinx-wood desk. His long snout was poking into a copy of *The Deathbringer*, Swerdlingham's local newspaper.

'According to the financial pages,' he said in a satisfied voice to a plump blue chicken who was perching on a nearby coffee table, pecking at a handful of seed scattered across it, 'it seems that Slangfash Industries is once again the market leader in the conference and leisure sectors in this part of the galaxy, beating our nearest rival by over fifteen per cent of market share.'

The blue chicken raised its beak from its seed. 'This is pleasing news,' it squawked in a high, self-important voice, 'but we must not become complacent. To thrive, a company must diversify into new areas. We should be thinking about fresh products to launch under the Slangfash brand – weaponry, instruments of torture, pens, mugs, et cetera, et cetera...'

The Blue Chickens of Brocklesbane were one of the few alien species tolerated by the Swerdlixian Lizard Swarm. The lizards, while fearsome warriors and superb military strategists, were a bit rubbish when it came to everyday stuff like ordering stationery and paying the gas bill – anything, in short, that wasn't to do with blowing things to bits. To relieve this problem, they had

formed an uneasy alliance with the blue chickens of the neighbouring star system of Brocklesbane, who carried out most of the boring little jobs the Swerdlixian Lizards were far too busy conquering and killing to do for themselves. In return, the blue chickens received a cut of all the wealth plundered by the lizards. Some of the shrewder blue chickens, like the one now in Admiral Gecko's office, had even wormed their way into the higher echelons of lizard society as advisers.

'Great idea,' said Admiral Gecko. 'Maybe we could create a range of Slangfash leisure wear – jumpers and cardigans and so forth. Comfortable, hardwearing, yet at the same time deeply terrifying.'

The blue chicken clucked its approval.

'A splendid suggestion. We should carry out some market research to determine—'

There was a sudden knock at the door.

Admiral Gecko put down his paper.

'Funny,' he said. I'm not expecting any visitors.'

'Shall I send them away, Lord Admiral?' asked the blue chicken.

'Yes, tell them to do one. We're busy.'

'At once.'

The blue chicken hopped off the coffee table and waddled towards the office door. It had taken only a few steps when the office door suddenly exploded in a white-hot ball of flame. The blue chicken squawked in alarm, laid an egg, and staggered backwards as sparks and fragments of charred wood rained down all around it.

111

Admiral Gecko leaped to his feet. 'What in the name of Kyross. . . ?'

The smoke around the singed remains of the door frame cleared, revealing the silhouette of a tall, imposing figure. Its long tail coiled and uncoiled a few times, like a slowly clenching fist.

'Good afternoon,' said the figure.

'Whaaa–? Who. . . ?' stammered Admiral Gecko.

The figure strode into the room, revealing itself to be a Swerdlixian Lizard of immense size, clad in the finest and most expensive war-jerkin and battle-pants money could buy. Its green scales shone like polished armour. On its face, it wore a sneer filled to the brim with contempt and loathing. Wisps of smoke curled from its nostrils.

'Admiral . . . Skink?' whispered Admiral Gecko. 'You're back! Oh, praise the Lizard God himself! You're alive!'

Admiral Skink chuckled and popped a Dysonian sparkworm into his mouth.

'Yes indeed,' he said. 'But I'm not sure I'd be quite that happy about it if I were you.'

Skinketta looked up from her reception desk in the lobby of Slangfash Palace, where she'd spent the past half-hour failing to complete the crossword in that morning's *Deathbringer* and picking her nose, to see Admiral Skink striding towards her. How impressive the Admiral looked in his newly regrown body, she reflected. A glorious new era of the Swerdlixian Lizard Swarm was at hand.

'How did your meeting with Admiral Gecko go?' she asked.

Admiral Skink winked. 'Let's just say Admiral Gecko has rethought his career path and taken up an exciting new position as a heap of smoking ashes.' He chuckled and took a big bite out of a hunk of white meat he was holding in one claw. He offered it to Skinketta. 'Brocklesbane fried chicken?'

'Perhaps later. I have done what you asked, O Scaly Tyrant, and discovered what the new extension to the palace is being used for. A certain construction project is taking place there.'

Admiral Skink's greeny-yellow eyes widened expectantly. 'And. . . ?'

'And,' continued Skinketta, 'I think that you are going to like it a lot.'

'Excellent! But first, dear niece, we have a sad duty to attend to.' Admiral Skink reached into an inside pocket and drew out a long green object. It was as stiff as a stick of French bread. He placed it on the reception desk. 'This is Pickles. The loyal Thrall-Beast who selflessly housed my mind for these past few months of imprisonment on the planet Earth. Sadly, with my mind returned to its

rightful place, Pickles's body is now no more than an empty husk. I owe a debt of gratitude to this brave little reptile and we should take a moment now to give thanks for his noble sacrifice.' Admiral Skink closed his eyes and clasped his great clawed hands together over the motionless body of the little iguana. 'O Kyross, Great Lizard God, we commend to you this little Thrall-Beast, whose services in the cause of evil were so steadfast and so–'

'Uncle!' said Skinketta in a breathless voice.

'Don't interrupt me, girl,' said Admiral Skink. '. . . Whose service in the cause of evil was so steadfast,' he continued, 'and so befitting of a creature who–'

'Uncle!' hissed Skinketta again.

'What on Swerdlix is it?' demanded Admiral Skink.

'Look!'

'Huh?'

Admiral Skink opened his eyes and was astonished to find Pickles the iguana very much alive and well and stretching his scaly green limbs across the reception desk as he opened his mouth and emitted a long, high-pitched yawn.

'Pickles!' cried Admiral Skink.

'Hello, My Lord,' said the little lizard sleepily in his scratchy voice. 'That was a long sleep. What planet are we conquering today?'

CHAPTER SEVEN
HIDEOUS MONSTERS

Passing through the wormhole, Lance had expected swirling colours and raging vortices, a spectacular, breakneck tumble into the unknown – in other words, the opening titles of *Doctor Who*.

What he got was an uncomfortable wriggle through a tight black tube towards a single bright point of light.

'Now I know how the cheeseburger I had for tea last night feels,' he mused.

'Thanks for that image,' muttered Tori, wriggling along behind him.

As the point of light neared, the black tunnel took an unexpected dip and Lance and Tori suddenly felt themselves sliding uncontrollably towards it. Screaming, they plummeted headlong through the darkness. There was a detonation of blinding white light and then a monumental squelch.

When the breath had returned to his body, Lance opened one eye and took in his surroundings.

'We've arrived,' he whispered. 'We're actually on another planet!'

Tori opened her eyes.

'Yuck!'

119

'Yeah, not actually all that impressive, is it?'

They were sitting in a largish metal container with four rusty walls. Above them was a rectangle of blue sky laced with thin strips of white cloud. The container was half-filled with soggy bits of cardboard, rotting fruit, fish skeletons and some kind of disgusting pink and red slime, the origin of which they didn't want to think about.

Lance looked around. 'This must be some kind of waste disposal module,' he said finally.

'It's a skip, isn't it?' replied Tori. 'Don't try and dress it up in fancy sci-fi language, Lance. We've landed in a skip.'

'Yeah. We're in a skip,' admitted Lance. 'Explains where that trash-eating Thrall-Beast came from. He must have wandered back up the wormhole before it closed.'

They got to their feet and peeped over the top of the skip. Half a second later, they ducked back down inside it.

'Wowee!' said Lance. 'That's a bit more like it!'

'Definitely an alien planet, then!' said Tori.

'Yep. One with blue chickens and giant insecty things.'

'And an awful lot of very mean-looking lizard-creatures.'

'They must be the lizards of the Swerdlixian Swarm. At least that proves we're on the right planet,' said Lance.

'Wowee!' said Tori again.

'I agree,' said Lance. 'Wowee!'

Tori suddenly gasped and grabbed Lance's arm.

'Oww! What is it?'

'Look!'

Tori pointed into a corner of the skip. Two enormous lizard-like creatures were staring straight at them, their giant mouths hanging open in hungry leers.

'Oh,' said Lance. He smiled at them. 'Erm, hello. We're . . . new here.'

The two lizards said nothing.

'Please don't eat us,' said Tori. 'We're very stringy and I bet we taste horrible. Lance here hasn't had a shower in three days so it's probably best not to eat him purely from a health and safety point of view.'

'Hey!' objected Lance. 'I shower every day, as it happens!'

Tori rolled her eyes. 'I'm trying to save your life, you moron,' she hissed at him from out of the corner of her mouth.

If the state of Lance Spratley's personal hygiene mattered to either of the two lizard-creatures, it did not register on their faces. Indeed, neither of the creatures had moved so much as a single millimetre since Lance and Tori had first clapped eyes on them.

'Bit . . . quiet, aren't they?' said Tori.

'I wonder. . .' muttered Lance. He picked up

123

a long, thin cardboard tube protruding from a nearby clump of rubbish. Very, very gently, he prodded the nearer of the lizard-creatures with it.

'What are you doing, you freak?' squeaked Tori. 'You'll get us killed!'

But, rather than rearing up like an angry crocodile and tearing the hapless boy to shreds in a blaze of reptilian fury, the lizard-creature merely crumpled up like a sheet of cellophane and lay motionless. Lance prodded the other lizard-creature and it too imploded into a crinkly heap like a scaly carrier bag.

'Ha!' exclaimed Tori and clapped her hands together. 'They're just empty skins! The Swerdlixians must shed their skins like snakes!'

Lance gathered them up. 'I've got an idea,' he said as he handed one of the skins to Tori and grinned. 'Here. This one matches your eyes.'

A few minutes later, clad in their lizard-skin disguises, Lance and Tori were walking down Swerdlingham High Street, their eyes popping with wonder at the sights they were seeing. Everywhere they looked were strange creatures – giant insects, strange blue birds, and lizards of all sizes – all of them doing strange things, many of them in very strange trousers.

A huge red sun hung in the pale sky, casting its baking glow over the city's low stone buildings and dust-covered rocky roads. In the distance loomed the menacing form of a huge conical tower the colour of blood.

The lizard skins were a snug fit, but incredibly hot. Fortunately, the eye-holes were big enough to afford them both a reasonable view. Several Swerdlixian Lizards nodded politely as they passed, and Lance and Tori guessed that the disguises must be working.

'I must admit,' said Tori in a loud whisper, 'when I woke up this morning I didn't think I'd be doing this today.'

'Same here,' hissed Lance. 'But I'm glad I am. Beats sitting at home waiting for a giant rock to fall on you.'

'So where do we go? What do we do? I take it you have a brilliant plan worked out?' asked Tori.

'You're joking, aren't you?' said Lance. 'I hadn't worked out anything beyond

126

guessing Admiral Skink's password. I guess we need to, you know, save the world and stuff again. Somehow.'

'What I think you mean,' said Tori, 'is that we need to find some of this flooblescoop shrub to make the lizard that ate your sister sneeze. Then find some fabulous alien super-weapon to blow up Asteroid Peach. And then find someone who can open up a new wormhole to get us home. All within the next – ooh – twelve hours or so.'

'Yeah, I was just going to say that, actually,' said Lance.

'Yeah, right.'

A scream tore through the air.

It was unlike any scream either of them had heard before, a piercing, warbling screech, the sort of sound a motorboat engine would

make if it had just seen the ghost of another, long since deceased, motorboat engine. Lance and Tori hurried around the corner and found themselves face to face with the source of the noise.

Three enormous insect-creatures, each the size of a human being, were involved in some sort of argument with a giant metal crab. The metal crab was gesticulating with one of its huge, savage pincers at a nearby low, hut-like structure made of woven reeds. The insect-creatures were waving their arms (or was it legs? they seemed to have a great many of both) madly and trying to shoo the metal crab away, making a frightful racket as they did so.

'I think that crab thing wants to demolish their home,' whispered Tori.

In an instant, Lance realised she was right.

The metal crab was not alive, or even a robot, but a machine akin to a bulldozer or JCB. There was a transparent dome set into its carapace within which Lance could make out a small Swerdlixian Lizard wearing a manic, spiteful expression on its stubby, sneering snout. Lance also saw now that the insect-creatures were a family. Two were tall, with long, bristling limbs and antennae, while the third was smaller and less developed. *Mum, Dad and Insect Junior,* he thought.

'Come on,' said Tori. 'We've got to help them!'

Lance opened his mouth. Words like 'idiotic', 'foolhardy' and 'none of our flipping business' were jostling for position his mind. But by the time he had assembled them into a sentence, Tori had already gone.

CHAPTER EIGHT
TELEPATHIC ICE CREAM

'You're joking!' spluttered Lance. 'We haven't got time to get mixed up in other people's business! We've got to save Earth from total destruction and Sally from being a giant lizard's dinner, or had that slipped your mind?'

Tori didn't reply. Instead, she ran towards the metal crab waving her arms and yelling,

as she tried to draw its attention away from the insects and their house.

Tori lived with her Aunt Hazel in a house filled with sick and injured animals that Hazel just couldn't resist bringing home and trying to help. So, just like her aunt, Tori was a sucker for a creature with a hard-luck story. Even, it seemed, a six-foot-tall alien insect-creature with masses of waggling antennae and limbs. Lance sighed and hurried after her.

The metal crab made a savage lunge at Tori with one pincer. Tori sidestepped nimbly and the pincer sliced through the air mere centimetres from her face.

'Hey!' called Lance to the crab. 'Over here, you cretinous crustacean!'

The metal crab swung its body around to face Lance. Lance saw the lizard within the

machine's cockpit laughing wildly. The crab shot its right pincer towards him, snapping like the jaws of a ferocious dog. Lance leaped backwards and the pincers slammed shut, barely missing his chest.

Tori jumped in front of the crab's left pincer. She waved her arms and the pincer shot towards her. Then Lance yelled again and the metal crab faltered, unsure whom to go for. The lizard inside clawed madly at its control levers, looking from Lance to Tori in indecision. Then they both yelled at once. The lizard pulled back hard on the control levers and both pincers shot towards their targets simultaneously with tremendous speed. There was a ripping, splintering sound and the metal crab suddenly split in two like an Easter egg, each half toppling over and

crashing to the ground. The Swerdlixian Lizard sat suspended in thin air for a moment, a look of extreme confusion on its face, before dropping heavily to the ground with a grunt of pain. It shook a scaly fist at them, bellowed something unintelligible in its own language, then turned its tail and scuttled away.

Before Lance and Tori had even got their breath back, the three insect creatures descended on them and smothered them in a series of joyful, multi-limbed hugs. They wailed and hollered in their strange rasping voices. Lance and Tori thanked them politely but it was clear the insects couldn't understand a word they were saying.

The smaller of the insects suddenly made a loud clicking noise with one of its many hands. It scurried over to a nearby market

stall and tossed a weird alien coin at the insect-creature in charge. The stallholder, a much older insect-creature with faded grey mandibles, handed over two objects, which the small insect-creature brought over and handed to Lance and Tori. The children took the objects and stared at them in disbelief. They looked shockingly familiar.

'Ice-cream cornets?' said Lance.

'Alien ice-cream cornets!' said Tori.

'Should we eat these?' asked Lance, nervously. 'They might turn us into creatures like them. Or at the very least they might contain all sorts of alien bacteria to which we have no immunity.'

'On the other hand,' said Tori, eyeing the family of insect-creatures who were now staring at them in obvious expectation,

'it would be rude not to.'

Lance shrugged and tasted his ice cream, feeding it carefully through the mouth of the lizard skin. 'Sort of mango-ish,' he said brightly. 'Not bad, actually!'

Tori tried hers. 'Mmmm!'

The insects rattled their limbs and wailed appreciatively.

And then a strange thing happened, as if enough strange things hadn't already happened to Lance and Tori that day. The indecipherable wailing and rasping of the insect-creatures suddenly transformed itself into recognisable speech. Lance and Tori gasped.

'Most kind! Most kind! Truly, you are wise and fair,' said one of the larger insects in a distinctly female voice.

135

'Such a generous and noble pair of lizards! You do us great honour!' said the other large insect in a formal-sounding male voice.

'Cheers! That was well good!' said the small insect in what sounded to Lance and Tori like the voice of a teenage boy. It was very odd to hear it emerging from the insect's mouth.

'We can understand you!' cried Lance in awe.

''Course you can, you plonker,' said the small insect. 'Telepathic ice cream, innit? Everyone here uses it. It lets all the different species communicate with one another.'

'Wowee!' said Tori. 'Amazing! How does it work?'

'Well,' replied the small insect. 'I could stand here all day explaining to you how telepathic ice cream works – or we could get you two human beings inside the house before any

real lizards spot you and zap you into very small pieces. Which would you rather?'

'The first one, please,' said Lance and Tori together.

Inside, the insects' house was surprisingly roomy. The reeds that formed their home were cool to the touch and created a calming atmosphere. The insects showed Lance and Tori to a sofa-like structure made of large yellow leaves and the two children sat down.

'First, some introductions,' said the small insect. 'I'm Wayne and this is my mum and dad: Doreen and Philip.'

The two older insects waved their antennae in greeting.

'Hello, my loves,' said Doreen.

'Charmed to meet you,' said Philip.

Both seemed much less imposing and formal now they were in their own home.

'Wayne, Doreen and Philip?' asked Lance. 'That doesn't sound very . . . alien.'

'The telepathic ice cream you ate is translating our names into their Earth equivalents,' said Wayne. 'Our actual names are **Wwwwwwwwwwwggwwwwwwwwaayh, Daaaaaaaaaaaahhaaaaaaaaaaaaaaaarah,** and **Phillllllllllllllllllllllllllddllllllllllllllllllllllllllllll,** but they're probably a bit hard to pronounce with your non-insect mouthparts. We're Ewargi.'

'E-whatty?' blinked Lance.

'Ewargi,' said Wayne. 'Our species used to rule Swerdlix centuries ago. Beautiful, this planet used to be – lush forests, meadows, waterfalls, the whole bit. But then our sun

138

started getting bigger – and hotter. It's quite an old star, you see, and that's what happens to them. As the sun got hotter, all the lizards that lived here too thrived in the heat and started getting bigger. And meaner! Most of the forests and greenery died away because the planet was too hot and eventually we ended up with this dusty old dump you see today. The lizards got so big and so mean that they took over the planet from us.'

'That's terrible!' gasped Tori, shaking her head.

Philip shrugged. 'Ah well. That's evolution for you. We still love this place, though. It's our home. And we got off lightly compared to most species the lizards encounter. At least they tolerate our presence and don't just destroy us.'

'But why?' asked Lance. 'What's so special about you?'

Doreen let out a peculiar warbling chuckle. 'Food!' she said with glint in her huge insect eye. 'It's a well-known fact that Ewargi make the best food in the galaxy and, since no Swerdlixian Lizard can cook to save his life, if they want to carry on enjoying our Sky Walrus burgers and Scramthorn flans, they have to keep us around.'

'So why was that lizard trying to knock your house down?' asked Tori.

'He wants the land it's on,' replied Philip. 'We live very close to the main marketplace. It's a prime area.'

'He wants to set up a kiosk selling Tailnipper Mites,' explained Doreen. 'They're little creatures who eat up the lizards' old bits of skin and scales. Keeps them well groomed.

You can make lots of money selling them as the lizards here prize them above all things. Except wanton destruction,' she added bitterly.

'But you are good lizards,' said Philip. 'I can tell. Not like the Swerdlixian ones you so outwardly resemble. You have kind hearts.'

'Newsflash, Mum and Dad!' said Wayne. 'These are not lizards. They're humans from Earth wearing old shed lizard skins as a disguise. Look!'

And with that, Wayne reached out with a couple of his segmented limbs and pulled the skins off Lance and Tori's heads as if they were no more than the hoods on a couple of anoraks.

Lance and Tori smiled sheepishly at their hosts.

'Monsters!' cried Philip. 'Hideous monsters!'

142

'Don't eat us, I beg you!' pleaded Doreen.

'They're not going to eat us,' said Wayne, rolling his enormous multifaceted eyes. 'You'll have to forgive, Mum and Dad, guys,' he said to Lance and Tori. 'They're a bit old-fashioned. Never met anyone from Earth before, you see.'

'How do you know we're from Earth? In fact, how do you even know about Earth?' asked Lance.

'Know all about you, don't I?' said Wayne. He opened a pouch that was slung over one of his many shoulders and drew out a magazine. 'You're in here, see? *Species of the Universe Monthly!* I get it by mail order from Alpha Centauri. Tells you all about different alien races. Human beings are my favourite creatures. After the Pentaxian Slop-Beetle.'

CHAPTER NINE
A SINGLE, SOMEWHAT ANCIENT, UNWRAPPED TOFFEE

'Morning, dear!'

'Morning, dear!'

Mr and Mrs Spratley were sprawled on the huge, comfortable back seat of the Prime Minister's limo. He had offered it to them as somewhere to sleep while he worked through the night to solve the pressing problem of Sally Spratley being trapped

in an alien creature's insides.

Mr Spratley yawned. In his hand he found he was still holding Lance's note explaining that he and Tori had gone through the wormhole. He stared at it. 'Do you know, love,' he said, 'over the past few months I haven't felt like myself at all.'

'Really?' said Mrs Spratley. She rubbed her eyes.

'Yes,' said Mr Spratley. 'I'm all sort of relaxed. Stuff doesn't bother me so much these days.'

'Same here,' said Mrs Spratley. 'Yesterday a brush salesman came to the door and I invited him in for a cup of tea! A few months ago I would have told him to clear off and hit him on the back of the head with one of his demonstration models.'

'The only thing that makes me angry,'

145

said Mr Spratley, 'is the thought of Lance and Sally being in danger. Isn't that odd?'

'Me too!' agreed Mrs Spratley. 'Nowadays when I look at the kids I don't even feel ashamed or annoyed! I just want them to be happy. It's very strange.'

'I went to see Doctor Hoyle about it,' admitted Mr Spratley, 'but when I told him he just laughed.'

Mrs Spratley tutted. 'He's always been useless, that Doctor Hoyle. We should get a second opinion.'

The Prime Minister awoke with a start, finding himself slumped against a tree, his mouth dry. An eager sun had already risen and seemed to be directing its rays directly into his bleary eyes. He checked his watch,

squinting: nearly seven a.m. Had he been at home at 10 Downing Street, he thought bitterly, his housekeeper would be waking him up about now with a cup of Earl Grey, a cupcake and a freshly ironed copy of *The Times*. A little way off, behind the stage on which sat the so-called omega wave projector, the Prime Minister could see shapes stirring within his limousine. The Spratleys would be out and about and looking for him soon, demanding an update.

Unfortunately, he had no news with which to update them.

Or, even more unfortunately, any plan for how to get some.

Oh, and the world was going to end, too. *Mustn't forget that,* he thought with a now-familiar sinking feeling. Although, it was hard

to forget that when everybody was blaming him just because he had claimed to be able to stop it happening, but, as it turned out, couldn't.

The Prime Minister heaved a sigh and wished he had been born into a simpler life, like that of a field mouse, or a member of the Opposition.

On a hunch, he slid a hand into the inside pocket of his jacket. There he found a smooth, hard lump. He drew it out, revealing a single, somewhat ancient, unwrapped toffee. He picked off a few bits of fluff and popped it in his mouth. Cogs in his brain began to turn, kick-started by the sugar.

He suddenly remembered something his father had told him when he was a boy. It was during a game of draughts, when he

had kept his father waiting for minutes, unable to decide which piece to move, paralysed by anxiety and indecision. 'Jarvis Horatio Edgar St. John Pocket. You are a ditherer, boy!' his father had often told him. 'A panicky, indecisive ditherer! If you cannot keep your head when all about you are losing theirs, you shall grow up a prize fool and amount to very little. Make your move, boy! Any move! But make it decisively and stand by it!'

His father was always saying stuff like that. Even today. The elder Mr Pocket was a computer programmer by trade, specialising in the development of encryption codes for industry and–

WHUMP!

The toffee shot out of the Prime Minister's

149

mouth like a bullet as he gave a great spluttering gasp of shock and excitement. He had just had an absolute corker of an idea! As the idea sank in he watched, amazed, as the toffee ricocheted off a nearby tree, startling a passing squirrel, before clattering onto the footpath. Then that gave him another idea, and that was another absolute corker, too!

He allowed himself a tiny triumphant chuckle.

A few hours later, Mr and Mrs Spratley stood listening with sceptical expressions and folded arms as the Prime Minister outlined his plan. Or rather, his plans. He seemed very keen to point out that he had two, and that they were both, apparently, corkers.

It was a fine day in Hyde Park. The members of the crowd who had not been frightened away by the appearance of the purple lizard-creature had stuck around to see what would happen next and lay dotted around, sleeping under their coats, like travellers delayed overnight at an airport. The sudden whir of approaching helicopter blades made them peer into the sky curiously.

The Prime Minister led the Spratleys over to the stage, where an elderly gentleman with a fierce moustache was hunched over a vast and complex bank of computer equipment. Wires, leads and cables of every variety sprouted from the equipment and fed into the laptop computer that Admiral Skink had used to program the non-omega-wave-projecting omega wave projector.

'Allow me to introduce my father,' said the Prime Minister, tapping the elderly man on the shoulder.

Mr Pocket straightened up, moustache bristling, and shook hands heartily with Mr and Mrs Spratley. 'Christopher Pocket,' he growled. 'Pocket Technology. Pleased to meet you.'

'These are the Spratleys,' said the Prime Minister. 'The poor family whom we are so keen to–'

'Yes, yes. Let me explain to these good people what we're doing here,' said Mr Pocket, interrupting his son. 'Time is of the essence, Jarvis, and we can't stand around all day jabbering, eh? What we need is decisive action!'

The Prime Minister opened his mouth and then closed it again. He nodded.

Mr Pocket jerked a thumb at his computer equipment. Mr and Mrs Spratley stared at it uncomprehendingly. 'This little lot may not look very impressive to the untrained eye,' said Mr Pocket. 'But it is in fact the most sophisticated piece of code-breaking computer equipment ever devised. The T-250! This computer is the envy of NASA and every

153

government and mathematician in the world. It can calculate over a billion combinations of letters and numbers every second. Whatever password or encryption this devilish space lizard has placed upon the controls of his machine, the T-250 here shall discover with extreme rapidity, mark my words!'

Mr Spratley beamed appreciatively. He nudged his wife. 'Ooh, that sounds good, doesn't it, dear?'

Mrs Spratley sniffed. 'Maybe. And then what?'

'And then,' said Mr Pocket, 'we shall be able to pass through the wormhole to the lizard's own planet.'

'Not so much we, of course,' the Prime Minister chipped in, 'as the battalion of troops I have standing by. They have orders to capture Admiral Skink and return him here,

154

whereupon he shall be forced to use his superior technological know-how to divert the asteroid. Either that or the troops will find some other being on the other side of the wormhole who can assist us. There will be a separate battalion with the order to find and rescue your son and his friend Tori, transporting them safely home.'

'Good idea, eh?' said Mr Pocket. 'Looks like my son has taken firm and decisive action. For once in his life! Ha!'

The Prime Minister laughed weakly. 'Thanks a bunch, Dad,' he muttered under his breath.

'Hear that, love?' said Mr Spratley. 'They'll soon have our darling son returned to us.'

'But how does all this help Sally?' said Mrs Spratley, raising her eyebrows. 'None of this fancy computer business is going to get

my daughter out of that thing!' She jabbed a finger at the enormous form of the long-necked purple lizard-creature slumbering nearby, a look of almost moronic contentment on its long, scaly face as it snored and dreamed about whatever purple lizard-creatures dream about. Flies, presumably.

The Prime Minister flashed a fair attempt at a smile. 'This is where my second corker of a plan comes in. Observe the approaching helicopter!'

Mr and Mrs Spratley gazed into the sky and saw an extraordinary sight. A large military-style helicopter with two enormous rotor blades was zooming through the clear morning air towards them. Dangling from a harness at the end of a long cable attached to the helicopter's belly was a large, bulky shape that they found strangely familiar.

For an absurd second, Mr Spratley thought it was an elephant, but then the realisation struck him and he let out a gasp of delight.

'It's the dinosaur!' he yelled. 'The tricera-whatsit!'

'Indeed it is!' said the Prime Minister, not bothering to disguise the smug tone in his voice.

'And what use is that going to be?' asked Mrs Spratley as the helicopter drew closer. The triceratops's four squat feet barely

cleared the top of Marble Arch, and a look of considerable displeasure crossed the creature's bony, three-horned face. A crowd of onlookers pointed with wonder at the dangling dinosaur.

'It's all to do with a toffee,' said the Prime Minister.

'Go on,' said Mrs Spratley with a roll of her eyes, arms still crossed. 'This better be good.'

'Well,' the Prime Minister began gleefully, 'I was eating a toffee, you see, and as I was chewing it I suddenly got the idea that my father, who is really quite the expert when it comes to code-breaking, and who has probably the best computer in the world for that very purpose—'

'The T-250!' chipped in Mr Pocket.

'Quite,' said the Prime Minister. 'The T-250. Hence he would be the ideal person to take a crack at unlocking the controls of Admiral Skink's device here. And I was so shocked and surprised at coming up with that idea that the toffee flew out of my mouth – POW! – just like that, you see?'

Mrs Spratley frowned so hard you could have grated cheese on her forehead.

But then Mr Spratley clicked his fingers. 'So you think the dinosaur could give a similar kind of shock to the monster that ate Sally?'

'Nail on head, Mr Spratley,' said the Prime Minister with a wink. 'I'm quite sure that when the purple beast that has swallowed your dear child sees the triceratops squaring up to it, horns raised and a fearsome snarl upon its face, it will spit out the young lady without delay.'

Mrs Spratley cocked her head to one side. 'It's worth a try. I'll give you that.'

'Excellent!' said the Prime Minister. 'Excellent! Well, no time to lose, eh?' He lifted a walkie-talkie to his lips and spoke. 'Hello? Are you receiving me, Captain Hill?'

The walkie-talkie crackled. 'Loud and clear, sir,' replied a confident voice. 'About to move into position. Where do you want the triceratops?'

'In front of that other massive reptile, please. The purple long-necked fellow over by the stage. You see it?'

'We have visual, sir,' said Captain Hill.

The Prime Minister frowned. 'Is that a fancy way of saying yes?'

There was a pause. 'Yes,' admitted Captain Hill. After another pause he asked, 'How

close do you want us to place this beast to the purple one, sir?'

'Oh,' said the Prime Minister. 'I hadn't thought of that. Erm. . .'

Mr Pocket looked up from the T-250 and snorted. 'Don't dither for heaven's sake, Jarvis. Tell the man what he needs to know!'

'I am not dithering,' said the Prime Minister between gritted teeth.

'You are dithering!' taunted his father again. 'Make your move and stand by it, boy!'

'One hundred and fifty metres!' shouted the Prime Minister into the walkie-talkie as he glared at his father. 'I want you to place the triceratops exactly one hundred and fifty metres in front of the purple lizard? Do you hear me, Captain Hill? One hundred and fifty metres and not a millimetre more or less.

161

And do it now!'

'Yes, sir.'

'Right now!'

'Yes, sir. We'll just swing the 'copter around so that the triceratops will be facing the purple creature.'

'I said NOW!!!'

There was a sudden deafening bang.

The Spratleys let out a gasp. The helicopter had turned so quickly in the air that the triceratops hanging beneath it had been swung backwards on its cable like the world's biggest conker. The cable had touched an overhead power line, causing an explosion, sending out a shower of white sparks – and snapping the cable.

Mr and Mrs Spratley watched in horror as the triceratops plummeted towards the ground.

The Prime Minister's face froze as he saw where the triceratops was heading. 'Oh dear,' he said very quietly and dived for cover.

Everyone in the park gazed, dumbstruck as, with a sudden thunderous **BOOOOOMMMM,** the triceratops landed on top of Mr Pocket's T-250 computer, flattening it in an instant. The triceratops shook itself, gave a mighty roar and then galloped off into the distance.

'Nooooooo!' wailed Mr Pocket, gazing at the pile of smashed circuit boards and crushed microprocessors. 'That was the only T-250 in the world!' He stared at his son with eyes slitted with rage, flung his arms into the air with a howl of anger and stomped away, shaking his head.

The eyes of everyone in the park shifted slowly towards the Prime Minister.

The Prime Minister winced, put his hand over his eyes, and very slowly began to walk away, muttering very quietly to no one in particular about needing a holiday.

But with his hand across his eyes he failed to see the toffee he had spat out a few hours ago lying on the footpath. He slipped on it and skidded into a flowerbed, where he remained for some time.

CHAPTER TEN
BRILL STUFF

'Good morning,' rumbled an enormous Swerdlixian Lizard in faded blue battle-pants. 'This is Jermyk Swinegum bringing you a very special live edition of Swerdlingham Channel One's toughest, cruellest, meanest, violentest and horriblest tellygoggler programme, Brill Stuff!'

'Oh, not this loser,' muttered Wayne.

He took a handful of sweet-smelling dried leaves from a bowl on the nearby coffee table and dropped them into his mouth.

'Jermyk Swinegum might be a horrid, smug, idiotic poser,' said Doreen, 'but there's only a repeat of last night's *BeastEnders* on the other channel.'

'Silence, the pair of you,' commanded Philip. 'This is an important broadcast.'

The Ewargi family and the two children were sitting around the Ewargi's tellygoggler, which was a device exactly like an Earth television, except somehow made of twigs and spit. Lance and Tori had spent an uneasy night curled up on a couple of Wiffalinx tree bed-mats that their hosts had provided. Wiffalinx leaves, the Ewargi had assured them, were the most comfortable bedding material in the galaxy. But it still felt

to Lance like they were sleeping in a cutlery draw topped up with itching powder.

'And what a superb, historic day today truly is,' continued Swinegum. 'I'm reporting live from the new extension to Slangfash Palace where no less than a legend is about to reclaim his throne. Yes, this is the big one. Admiral Skink is back! And he's very graciously granted an interview to yours truly.'

The camera pulled back to reveal the imposing form of Admiral Skink standing beside Swinegum. Pickles the iguana was perching on Admiral Skink's shoulder like a pirate's parrot. They were in a huge metal room, something like an aircraft hangar.

'So that's what he really looks like!' said Lance, breathless, pointing at the image on the screen. 'The lizard who stole my brain!

167

Terrifying, isn't he?'

'Looks more like a moody newt to me,' said Tori with a sniff. She blinked. 'Hey! Wait a minute! That's Pickles, my iguana, there with him too!'

'Name-dropper,' muttered Doreen.

'Greetings, O Scaly Lizard Emperor!' bellowed Swinegum. 'Here at Brill Stuff! we're all massive fans of your violence and cruelty! We can't get enough of it.'

'Excellent!' said Admiral Skink and then suddenly Pickles poked Swinegum in the eye with his tail. Admiral Skink sniggered. 'There's some of that violence just for you. Did you enjoy it?'

'Erm, yes,' muttered Swinegum, rubbing his eye. 'It's an honour to have my eye poked by the Grand Ruler's Thrall-Beast.'

'Think nothing of it,' said Admiral Skink.

'Now,' said Swinegum, 'you've been away for a little bit, as we all know, but today you have at last returned to your adoring Lizard Swarm. Have you a message for them?'

'Indeed I do, Jermyk,' said Admiral Skink, 'but before I deliver it, allow me to do this. . .' He nodded at Pickles and the little iguana suddenly jabbed Swinegum's other eye with his tail. Pickles laughed his peculiar scratchy laugh.

'What an honour,' moaned Swinegum, 'to be poked in both eyes by the Grand Ruler's Thrall-Beast.'

Admiral Skink turned to face the camera.

'Now look here, inhabitants of Swerdlix,' he roared. 'In my absence, you've all gone as soft as the Fluffy Marshmallow Kittenoids of Comfyworld Three! We are supposed to be

169

the most fearsome race in the cosmos, not a bunch of spineless accountants and weedy sales executives! It seems to me that there has been a distinct lack of cowering obedience and terror around here since I've been gone. Well tonight, this will end!'

'What do you have in mind, O Wondrous Reptile Monarch?' asked Swinegum.

'Good question!' said Admiral Skink as Pickles suddenly poked Swinegum in each eye with his tail in quick succession. Swinegum howled with pain. 'Tonight I shall be launching my new starship, the *Dragonworm!*'

Admiral Skink motioned with his head and the camera panned across the scene, revealing a vast black metallic form. It was sleek and spiked, like an evil black Christmas tree laid on its side.

'This wondrous starship was a generous gift from my predecessor, the late and sorely missed Admiral Gecko. I have made several improvements and modifications and it is now undoubtedly the fastest, deadliest and most powerful starship in all creation!'

'How fantastic!' groaned Swinegum, blinking his sore eyes and shaking his head. He could now see three Admiral Skinks standing in front of him. 'What do you plan to do with it, O Mighty Iguana-faced Doombringer?' He cringed and shut his eyes tightly.

'Don't worry, Swinegum!' guffawed Admiral Skink. 'Pickles here isn't going to poke you in the eye again. Here to answer your question is my navigator and niece, the lovely Skinketta – who will poke you in the eye.'

'What– OOF!'

172

Swinegum suddenly found himself on the receiving end of a thwack to the eye that felt like a runaway rocket. He forced open his swollen eyelid to see a short, squat form looming over him, brandishing a fist. The short, squat form was grinning inanely.

'Well, it was really more a punch than a poke as it turned out,' grinned Admiral Skink. He patted Skinketta on her beefy arm.

'All right, mate?' growled Skinketta at Swinegum. She folded her arms and looked into the camera. 'Tonight, my uncle the Admiral and I will be taking the *Dragonworm* for a little spin and we will be blowing up random targets throughout the city. Just for a bit of fun.'

'Just to remind you all who's boss,' added Admiral Skink. 'A bit of casual horror and destruction will soon have everyone nicely in

173

shape for the next battle campaign. Then perhaps we can restore the Swerdlixian Lizard Swarm to its rightful place as supreme power in the universe.' He waved a clawed finger at the viewers. 'So remember, fellow Swerdlixian Lizards, I'm back, I'm meaner than ever, and I just might be blowing you up tonight. Have a lovely rest-of-the-morning. Now back to Jermyk Swinegum.'

Admiral Skink and his niece looked around but there was no one there. From the distance came the faint sound of running footsteps.

Philip reached out with a spindly limb and switched off the tellygoggler. 'Random targets?' he said bitterly. 'Yesterday a lizard was trying to evict us so I think we may safely bet that our house will be one of the

first places they destroy. O woe, woe, woe!'

'Yes! Woe, woe, woe!' joined in Doreen.

'Enough with the woeing,' said Wayne, still munching his leaves. 'You're depressing our guests.'

'Don't worry,' said Tori. 'We've got more than enough problems of our own.'

'Too right,' said Lance. 'We're millions of miles from home – which an asteroid is about to destroy, anyway – and my little sister is currently lodged within the throat of an enormous purple lizard-creature and it's up to us to rescue her by finding something called flooblescoop powder. In fact, you could probably say that in the problem department we are exceptionally well provided for.' He let out a sigh and slumped back on the sofa.

'Well, that last one's easy, at least,' said Wayne. He passed Lance a handful of the dried leaves.

Lance looked at them quizzically.

'Flooblescoop shrub leaves,' said Wayne with a wink of one of his huge compound eyes. 'S'what Dad sells on his market stall. Consider them a gift. As for your other problem – hands up anyone who has a totally brilliant idea for saving the planet Earth.'

The others stared at him dumbly.

Wayne raised a hand and laughed. 'Just me then?'

CHAPTER ELEVEN
THE MANTIS SEER'S PROPHECY

The fat red sun was sinking below the horizon of Swerdlix, casting long, spindly shadows across the city of Swerdlingham. A large crowd had gathered to watch the launch of the starship *Dragonworm*, partly out of curiosity, partly out of a desire not to be at home in case the *Dragonworm* called around later and blew it up. Lizards, blue chickens, Ewargi and several

other, rarer Swerdlixian species like Dodo-Stags and Striped Plinkplonks mingled in the still-humid evening air as the enormous doors of Slangfash Palace's extension slid apart and the mighty starship was trundled out on a ceremonial platform. The platform was decorated with colourful banners, flags and the heads of some of Admiral Skink's enemies (he had asked especially for the heads).

Pickles the iguana was jumping nimbly here and there, showing several important-looking lizards to seats at a viewing area from which they would witness the *Dragonworm* take to the skies for its maiden flight. As each one arrived, Pickles announced their presence over a small megaphone.

A haughty female lizard with exceedingly long claws approached.

178

'Lady Swipescratch!' proclaimed Pickles in his scratchy voice. 'Slayer of the Pandemonium Stoats of Exidrill. Vanquisher of the Stainless Steel Termites of Skrigg.' He motioned for her to take a seat.

Next came an extraordinary sight. Upon a large squeaky-wheeled trolley sat the fattest lizard (possibly the fattest creature of any kind) that Pickles had ever seen. He looked like a giant, scaly pea with eyes and a snout and wore an expression of absurd dignity and pride. In his tiny claws, he held a bag containing unidentifiable pink squishy things, which he lobbed into his mouth at regular intervals. Two exhausted-looking lizards, their muscles

179

straining with the effort, were pushing the trolley on which he quivered like some huge, offensive dessert. They halted the trolley in front of Pickles, leaning against it and panting.

'And now please welcome Archduke Scabwheel!' announced Pickles. 'Eater of the Terrible Pie Creature of Artigant, Devourer of the Delicious Chocolate Fiends of Broog, Scoffer of the Sacred Custard Tart of Kloft.'

Archduke Scabwheel waved an arm as thin as a toothpick. 'Thank you, thank you,' he warbled good-naturedly. 'Move me into place, underlings!' His two servants groaned and manoeuvred the trolley with difficulty into a suitable gap in the viewing area.

There were very few celebrities on Swerdlix. Those that existed were mainly once-honoured warriors from long-ago battle campaigns that

everyone had forgotten about. They were wheeled out every now and again (literally in the case of Archduke Scabwheel) to appear at functions such as this or to voice their approval for whatever tyrannical policies the current Grand Ruler had decided to foist upon the Swarm.

'Next,' declared Pickles, 'is the honoured niece of our very own Grand Ruler, the lovely Skinketta. Tonight Skinketta is sporting a stunning dress designed by Vortisplinth Elbowsplat from the Boutique Nebulae of Plipple. The dress is fashioned from the skins of over seventy Sabre-toothed Minks and stitched together with the nervous system of a Traitorous Lobster. The buttons are real Sky Walrus noses. Over eleven endangered species became extinct in the making of this outfit.'

Skinketta did not acknowledge Pickles Instead, she spat a lump of gristle on to the floor, pushed past an elderly lizard to get to her seat and then started throwing nuts at the other guests.

Near the prow of the starship *Dragonworm*, Admiral Skink was readying the huge bottle of Swerdlixian sparkling white wine that would be broken on the ship to celebrate its

launch. He did this by shouting at and kicking the underling, Private Fangspittle, who was doing the actual work. In a moment of panic, Private Fangspittle dropped the bottle, shattering it and splashing the ceremonial spacesuit Admiral Skink had donned for the occasion with fizzy white wine.

'A million apologies, O Cruel Tyrant of the Skies!' stammered Private Fangspittle. 'I will fetch a new bottle immediately.'

'No need,' said Admiral Skink cheerily. 'Instead of the bottle we'll smash you against the ship instead. Kindly tie yourself to the ceremonial ribbon.'

Private Fangspittle nodded meekly and obeyed.

A sudden commotion in the crowd drew Admiral Skink's attention.

'Make way! Make way!' called an ancient, reedy voice.

'Pickles!' called Admiral Skink. 'What's the disturbance?'

'It is a Mantis Seer,' replied Pickles through his megaphone, his scratchy voice carrying over the crowd. 'He says he has an important prophecy to deliver.'

Admiral Skink sighed. 'I suppose you'd better let him through, then. He might have something useful to tell us.'

Mantis Seers were a rare type of insect native to Swerdlix. They lived like hermits in the remotest desert areas and were supposed to be able to foretell the future. Rumour had it that they could communicate with individual grains of sand, and use the desert as a huge computer to work out

184

their predictions. Occasionally, a Mantis Seer would saunter into an inhabited area and announce that it had some terrible prophecy of doom to impart, usually while everyone else was busy trying to have a good time, spoiling the vibe considerably. Much to the annoyance of all who heard them, their prophecies always came true.

The Mantis Seer was tall and thin and wreathed in a long, black cloak. It swept through the crowd like an imperious breeze.

'Admiral Skink,' it intoned in an ancient, cracked voice. 'I am here to give you . . . a warning!'

Everyone within earshot gasped. Those not within earshot of the Mantis Seer's remark, but within earshot of the gasp, also gasped. *Something pretty gasp-worthy must have gone*

down to make everyone gasp like that, they thought. And they were right. You didn't warn Admiral Skink about anything. It was asking for trouble as surely as if you had gone into a trouble shop and slapped down an order on the counter for fifty kilos of prime fresh trouble, gift-wrapped to go.

Admiral Skink regarded the spindly figure of the Mantis Seer and raised his scaly, reptilian eyebrows at it.

'Oh, really?'

'Yes, really,' said the Mantis Seer gravely. 'A warning.'

'About anything in particular?' asked Admiral Skink. 'The universe is about to end? Watch out for loose shoelaces? Get a pension?'

'If you launch this starship tonight,' croaked the Mantis Seer, 'you will die!'

Everyone nearby gasped again and those who could only hear the gasp gasped too, not wanting to be left out, and asked those nearer the action what had happened to cause a second spate of gasping. Those behind those who had only heard the gasp, gasped to hear the second gasp, and asked the second lot of gaspers what they were gasping at. A rapid chain reaction of gasps and explanations spread throughout the entire gathering until every last creature had had the opportunity to know exactly what the Mantis Seer had said to Admiral Skink and to gasp at it.

187

While all this gasping and explaining was going on, the two underling lizards who had been pushing Archduke Scabwheel's trolley left their position and sauntered quietly towards the starship *Dragonworm's* entrance hatch...

'Can't you be a bit more specific?' Admiral Skink asked the Mantis Seer (once the gasps had died down). 'I mean, of course I'll die one day – everyone will – whether I launch this ship or not. So as predictions go, yours is, at best, a little imprecise.'

An awed hush fell across the crowd. How generous the Grand Ruler was being in conducting a civil conversation with this impertinent Mantis Seer, when he could so easily reduce him to ash with a single breath!

The Mantis Seer cocked its head to one side, and then stuck a spindly finger into the

188

dark recesses of its hood, presumably to scratch its chin thoughtfully.

'All right,' it said finally, 'how about this? If you launch this starship, within one hour of take-off a Two-Toed Antelope-Bat will be sucked into starboard engine number three by a freak gust of wind, causing a thirteen per cent loss of speed and preventing the ship from gaining sufficient altitude to clear the peak of Mount Jaggersplinch. The ship will crash on the north face of the mountain, near a little lake surrounded by golden spike-daisies. You will survive the crash, but on building a campfire to keep yourself warm while awaiting rescue, you will slightly scratch your right index claw. A vicious microscopic parasite native to the mountain will enter your bloodstream via the wound and release

chemicals into your system that will cause your feet to swell up to nearly twelve times their normal size, until they explode with the force of a hydrogen bomb, killing you and everyone within a radius of four Swerdlixian kilometres.' The Mantis Seer paused. 'There. That specific enough for you, mate?'

This revelation was followed by more gasps, more explanations and more secondary gasps.

Meanwhile Archduke Scabwheel looked around as best his obese frame would allow him. 'Where are my underlings?' he demanded. 'My back requires scratching.' He scanned the surroundings and caught sight of them at the *Dragonworm's* entrance hatch. They seemed to be fiddling with the locking mechanism. 'Hey!' he called. 'Stop that and get back over here immediately!'

But something felt wrong. He frowned at the two lizards and a sudden terrible realisation struck him, 'Wait a minute!' he yelled. 'You're not my usual underlings! You're impostors! What have you done with my underlings?'

But no one was paying any attention to the Archduke. They were too busy waiting to see how Admiral Skink would react to the Mantis Seer's revised prediction. He reacted by reaching out a scaly claw, grabbing the Mantis Seer by its scraggy, hooded neck and rattling it.

'Look here, buster,' growled Admiral Skink. 'That is without a doubt the most ridiculous thing I have ever heard and if you think for one nanosecond that I am taken in by it then you. . . '

Admiral Skink's voice trailed away and his jaw flopped open.

For as he shook the Mantis Seer's neck, its long black cloak fell away, revealing it to be not a Mantis Seer at all, but three Ewargi – Philip, Doreen and Wayne to be precise – balanced on each other's shoulders. Wayne, who was the uppermost of the stack, and whose neck was being held, smiled sheepishly.

Admiral Skink snorted. 'You have made a terrible, terrible mistake to mock me like this, Ewargi scum,' he hissed.

'I'll tell you one thing I do predict, Admiral,' said Wayne with a wink. 'Your starship's about to get nicked.'

'And I predict that you shall fry!' snarled Admiral Skink and popped a Dysonian Sparkworm into his enormous jaws. But before he could unleash his fiery breath, Doreen and Philip shoved handfuls of

flooblescoop leaves into his mouth. Admiral Skink released Wayne from his grip and sank to his knees, coughing and spluttering, a sickly pink smoke issuing from his nostrils.

'Time we weren't here,' muttered Wayne and he and his parents made a desperate dash towards the Dragonworm.

'Stop them!' yelled Pickles. 'Stop them right now!'

A gaggle of Swerdlixian Lizard security guards pelted after them, evil-looking disintegrator guns raised and ready to fire.

At the Dragonworm's entrance hatch, Archduke Scabwheel's mysterious underlings were still fiddling with the locking mechanism. One of them suddenly took hold of the skin under his chin and jerked it back over his head, revealing the sweating features of

193

Lance Spratley beneath.

'Blimey! It's boiling in here!'

'Get a move on!' hissed Tori, beside him. 'The Ewargi are coming! And so are a lot of very ticked-off-looking lizards!'

'I thought I'd be able to crack this locking mechanism easily,' complained Lance. 'You know how lazy Admiral Skink is. But it's quadruple-encoded with nineteen-digit numbers. It could take me billions of years to guess the right sequence.'

'Lance, we haven't got thirty seconds, never mind billions of years!' hissed Tori. 'Just try to think like Admiral Skink!'

The security guards were gaining on the Ewargi. Bright green bolts of light exploded from their disintegrator pistols, slicing through the air on every side of them. When

194

they got to the viewing platform, Wayne gave Archduke Scabwheel a tremendous push and the enormously fat lizard rolled off his trolley towards the security guards.

'Excuse me!' hollered the Archduke, his speed gathering. 'This is quite unacceptable! I was trying to drink a cocktail!'

With a terrific crash, Archduke Scabwheel smashed into the security guards like a big scaly bowling bowl, sending them flying in all directions.

'They're nearly here,' said Tori, tugging at the arm of Lance's lizard skin. 'Either you open the hatch now or we're all dead.'

'I can't do it,' muttered Lance. 'It's too complicated! Why would Admiral Skink make the locking mechanism so difficult? Even if you knew the correct codes it would take ages to enter them. It doesn't make sense!'

He slumped over the controls and felt his eyes wander upwards. He often raised his eyes to the ceiling like this in class when asked a particularly difficult question. His teachers loved to remind him that the answer was never 'up there'. Suddenly Lance's eyes alighted on a small red button set into the archway over the entrance hatch. He blinked at it. Hang on a minute. . .

Then he giggled.

'Find the prospect of imminent death funny, do you, Lance?' said Tori.

The security guards had picked themselves up and were even now training their weapons on the fleeing Ewargi family.

Lance giggled again and stabbed a finger at the small red button.

With a hiss and a clang, the hatch slid open.

'Wowee!' said Tori. 'You did it!'

'I should have realised,' chuckled Lance. 'The locking mechanism's just a decoy.'

He and Tori hurried inside the hatch.

'Room for three more?' asked Wayne, his long tubular tongue lolling out, as the three Ewargi finally arrived, their numerous limbs flailing.

'This reminds me of when we were young, eh Doreen?' said Philip. 'All this drama and running about.'

'I know what you mean,' replied Doreen. 'It's like that time we stole a space pirate's star freighter and spent a fortnight on the run from the galactic mafia.'

Philip chortled. 'Some honeymoon that was!'

'Blimey,' muttered Wayne looking from Doreen to Phillip. 'The things you learn about your parents. . .'

'All aboard!' cried Lance.

The three insects scurried inside and the hatch slammed shut. A moment later there was a sound like the sneezing of a thousand elephants and the starship *Dragonworm* shot into the air with ferocious speed. Soon it was little more than a speck vanishing into the darkening sky.

Amidst the crowd it left behind – many of whom had had to sit down and rest after all

the gasping they had done – Skinketta surveyed the faces of those present on the viewing platform in search of her uncle, but he was nowhere to be seen.

CHAPTER TWELVE

BY THE LIGHT OF THE
SILVERY ASTEROID

Back on Earth, in the clear blue sky of spring,
the sun had a rival.

The glistening, winking form of Asteroid Peach
no longer resembled a silvery biscuit crumb.
It had grown rapidly over the last two hours
until now it looked more like a dazzling silver
coin. It was surrounded by a brilliant halo of
white light that danced and glimmered like the

sun's corona during an eclipse. The light from Asteroid Peach shone down on the northern hemisphere of the planet, gifting everything it touched with a ghostly second shadow.

It twinkled on the shoppers in Cottleton High Street, for whom even the prospect of the end of the world was no reason to stop the ceaseless, almost primal, hunt for bargains. They bustled in and out of the shops and the indoor market, their eyes flitting no higher than the hats perching on the heads of the mannequins in PrimeCheap's window display.

It glittered on the house of Peach Maguire, the girl after whom this uninvited visitor to the planet had been named. Peach herself was inside, in her bedroom, boasting to her friends on the internet about how she had discovered the asteroid. No one believed her.

Even her closest friend, Jasmine Pepper, who was there at the time of the discovery, was refusing to admit it, just for the sheer fun of seeing Peach's frustrated reaction.

It sparkled on the factory roof of the Cottleton Desk Tidy Company while the workers inside continued doggedly with their daily tasks and tried not to think about whether there would be any desks in existence tomorrow to require tidying.

It glistened on the lone triceratops bounding up the hard shoulder of the M1 back towards Cottleton. As it galloped, the creature cast a small eye upwards at the asteroid and thought, in its slow, measured way, *Here we go again.*

It glimmered on dogs and cats, who even now, at this crucial point in Earth's history,

were no closer to settling their differences.

It gleamed on sparrows and robins and starlings and glowed on magpies who actually quite liked the look of the glittering silver object in the sky.

Across the Atlantic Ocean in New York, it shimmered on the city's new mayor, which had settled in nicely to its new home, and which, in its own uncomplicated way, was looking forward to a pleasant day's photosynthesising.

It blinked on the building that housed representatives of all the world's nations, who had finally decided who was sitting next to whom and how many sausages you were allowed to take from the buffet (two). But they didn't notice its pale unearthly light because a fresh dispute had broken out over whether girls were better than boys.

And, in London, it glinted on the scales of a strange, long-necked purple lizard-creature basking in the sunshine in Hyde Park. Trapped within the throat of the lizard-creature was a small, bored girl who was wishing she were elsewhere. A few comics, a Rubik's Cube and a torch had been forced down the lizard-creature's gullet in order to keep Sally Spratley occupied while a gang of white-coated scientists tried to free her. But the comics were ones she had read before and the stifling humidity within the creature's throat had caused all the coloured stickers to peel off the Rubik's Cube, rendering it useless. She wished her big brother were here so she could kick him, because that always made her laugh.

CHAPTER THIRTEEN
BLOOZLEQASH POISONING

The starship *Dragonworm* flashed through interstellar space like a sleek black dart fired into the heart of the night sky.

Aboard, on the ship's bridge, a large insect-creature lounged in the pilot's seat with several pairs of its spindly legs resting on the control console. It was shovelling dried flooblescoop leaves into its mouth.

205

'Yeah, they're a piece of cake to fly, these things,' Wayne was saying. 'They're ninety-nine per cent automated. Basically you just tell it where you want to go and then all you have to worry about is which of the in-flight music stations you want to listen to.' He flipped a switch on the console and a noise like a thousand tea trays falling into a volcano filled the air. 'Ganthorian Tapeworm Thrash!' shouted Wayne above the racket. 'My favourite! There's this band called Plinthclump, right, and they've got thirteen drummers—'

Philip flashed out an antenna and switched off the music with a deft flick. 'Nobody wants to listen to your awful music, Wayne. We have an important job to do helping our Earth friends.'

'Yeah, yeah,' muttered Wayne. 'No one said

we had to do it in silence, though.'

Lance and Tori had finally discarded their lizard-skin disguises and were sitting at a computer console in the bridge, studying a star chart.

Doreen meanwhile was admiring the décor. 'Made these warships much more comfortable these days, haven't they?' she said, running a hand over the luxurious energy vole-skin furnishings. 'If you're going to go into space and take part in wars and things and blow up people's cities, you might as well do it in comfort, mightn't you?'

'According to this,' said Lance, ignoring Doreen and tapping a finger on a display screen, 'travelling at near enough this ship's top speed, we can be back at Earth an hour or so before Asteroid Peach hits.'

'But do we have enough firepower to destroy it?' asked Tori. 'I mean, I know this ship looks pretty tough with all its macho spikes and stuff, but does it really have the ability to disintegrate an entire asteroid?'

Wayne waved a limb over a control panel. There was a pleasing computerised beeping sound. 'No worries' he said, studying a read-out. 'There's enough military capability in this thing to zap a whole planet to bits.' He grinned evilly. 'Not that we want to do that, of course.'

'Looks like we could actually succeed!' said Lance delightedly. 'We really can save the world!'

Wayne laughed. 'Well, I wouldn't count your blue chickens before they've hatched,

but yes, the outlook is good.'

'Go Knowledge Warriors!' cried Lance and held up his hand for Tori to high-five it.

Tori snorted. 'Yeah, right. Knowledge Warriors.' Lance looked crestfallen. Then she winked and returned the high-five. 'Come on, Lance. Let's see if there's any lunch to be had on this starship.'

'The galley is just through the far door and second on the left,' called Wayne. 'I noticed it on the way in.'

'I suppose on ships like this there'll be some amazing alien machine in it that provides high-nutrition space-food in capsule form, is there?' asked Lance.

'No,' said Wayne. 'But there's loads of pop and crisps.'

Lance and Tori's feet click-clacked against the metal floor of the corridor as they made their way towards the *Dragonworm's* galley. They paused to watch the universe whiz by through a porthole, the stars streaming past like frantic, burning meteors.

'Isn't it incredible?' said Tori. 'We're seeing something no human being has ever witnessed before. I feel so privileged.'

'You're joking aren't you?' said Lance with a snigger. 'Every science fiction film or telly show has a scene where the spaceship zooms through space like this. I know this is real but I feel like I've seen it a million times already.'

'You really know how to ruin the moment, don't you, you lamebrain?' snapped Tori. She shoved open the galley door and disappeared inside, shaking her head and tutting.

Lance groaned. Girls. Always going on about 'moments'. Then he heard Tori scream.

He pushed open the galley door, his heart hammering wildly, and saw Tori standing with her hands raised, a look of fear and dread on her face.

Two Swerdlixian Lizards stood at the far end of the galley; both were leering at Lance with hideous, slavering jaws, and both were pointing extremely nasty-looking disintegrator pistols straight at Tori.

One lizard was stocky and muscular, the other small and bristly, like a malevolent toilet brush. To Lance's astonishment, he recognised them.

'Sludgeclaw?' he said in amazement. 'And Whiptail? What are you two doing here?'

The lizards exchanged a startled glance.

211

"Ow does 'e know who we are?' whispered Sludgeclaw.

'Dunno!' piped Whiptail in his high voice. 'Never seen the creature before. Most odd!'

Lance clicked his fingers. 'Of course!' he said. 'The last time I met you, you weren't actually you, were you? Not the real you.'

Sludgeclaw blinked at him. 'Have you been drinkin'?'

'He must have been!' trilled Whiptail. 'He's babbling like a crazy fool!'

'What's going on?' hissed Tori. 'Do you actually know these things, Lance?'

Lance laughed. 'Well, technically I haven't met these two lizards before, but what I have met is two computer-generated copies of them. They were in the virtual world my mind was sent to when Admiral Skink took over my body.'

'Oh great,' said Tori. 'Then perhaps you can use your influence on your old mates to stop them pointing two enormous ray guns at us?'

'There's computer-generated copies of us knockin' about?' asked Sludgeclaw, suddenly interested.

'Yes,' said Lance. 'I hope you got paid a royalty for the use of your likeness.'

Again, Sludgeclaw and Whiptail exchanged a startled glance.

'No,' muttered Sludgeclaw. 'As it 'appens, we didn't. Make a note of that in your diary, Whippy. We should speak to our lawyers when we get back to Swerdlix about possible monies owin' from the creation of virtual duplicates of us.'

The smaller lizard produced a handheld electronic device from a pocket of its imperial war-jerkin and tapped away at its tiny keyboard.

'I've just written "lawyers",' said Whiptail, 'but that should be enough to remind me.'

'No, no,' said Sludgeclaw. 'Write "phone lawyers" or "speak to lawyers", otherwise we'll forget why we want to see them and end up killin' them out of force of habit, what with us being such violent psychopaths. Remember that time we were plannin' to go on that picnic and you wrote "baker's" in your diary because

214

we wanted to buy some fresh stippleberry buns? By the time we got to the baker's we'd forgotten why we were there and ended up devastatin' the whole shoppin' precinct before we remembered what we wanted.'

'And then we couldn't get the stippleberry buns,' trilled Whiptail, 'because we'd killed the baker and all his family. And that spoiled the whole picnic!'

'That's right,' said Sludgeclaw. 'So make sure you write a proper note in your diary this time. It saves a lot of messin' about later.'

'Will do,' chirped Whiptail and entered some more text in his electronic diary. 'I've written "phone lawyers about virtual copies". That should do it.'

'Nice one, mate,' said Sludgeclaw. He waved his disintegrator pistol at the two children.

'Now that's settled, perhaps you two disgustin' monkey creatures could tell us what on Swerdlix is going on here? Me an' Whippy were loadin' supplies aboard for the Admiral's maiden flight and before we know it, the ship's taken off with us still onboard.'

'Still onboard!' repeated Whiptail and giggled dementedly.

There was an uncomfortable pause.

'We're health inspectors!' cried Lance suddenly. 'We're employees of the Swerdlixian Food Standards Agency and we're taking this starship into quarantine because of a suspected outbreak of bloozlequash poisoning.'

'Bloozlequash poisonin'?' said Sludgeclaw. He narrowed his eyes. 'Sounds very nasty.'

'Very nasty!' repeated Whiptail. 'Yuck!'

'What is it again, exactly?' asked Sludgeclaw.

216

'Obviously, I do know. It's just ... erm ... slipped my mind at the moment.'

'It's horrible!' said Tori. 'It makes your brain turn to steam and your stomach turn to a wasps' nest. The pain is so excruciating that anyone who contracts it is automatically deported to another planet so their relatives don't have to hear their terrible cries of agony.'

'Eww,' said Sludgeclaw. 'I think we can well do without that, eh Whippy?'

'Too right!' chirped Whiptail and giggled madly again.

'Maybe,' said Sludgeclaw, 'me and Whippy could just take one of the ship's escape pods and nip quietly back to Swerdlix? We don't wanna be 'angin' about this place if there's bloozlequash poisonin' around.'

'I think we can discreetly allow that,' said

Lance. He looked at Tori. 'What do you say, Doctor Walnut?'

'I concur,' said Tori with a friendly wink at the two lizards. 'Leave now and no one need ever know you were here.'

'Thank you!' said Sludgeclaw. 'Thank you very much! Most kind! Come on, Whippy. Let's head for the escape pods.'

'Most kind!' said Whiptail and made a little bow.

'I'll just let the wife know I'll be home slightly later than normal,' said Sludgeclaw and drew out a communicator device from his pocket. He switched it on and a metallic voice rang out.

'This is an emergency message broadcasting on all frequencies and wavelengths! Admiral Skink's fabulous new starship the *Dragonworm* has been stolen by a pair of primates from

the planet Earth and a family of Ewargi. The starship must be returned at all costs! The thieves are to be captured alive so that Admiral Skink has a suitable length of time to think up a really horrible punishment! I repeat, this is an emergency message . . . '

Sludgeclaw turned off the communicator with a click and re-aimed his disintegrator pistol at Lance and Tori.

'Oh dear,' he cackled. 'I don't think you wanted us to hear that, did you?'

Whiptail burst into a deafening peel of giggles.

CHAPTER FOURTEEN
BREAKING BREAD

The small control bridge of the starship *Dragonworm* was now somewhat crowded. Three Ewargi and two human beings sat tied together in a circle on the floor, their backs to one another, while two Swerdlixian Lizards danced up and down, giggling and congratulating each other on their cleverness. And as they danced, they sang:

Who slew the Treeshrews of Vega?

Who conquered the Ice Wolves of Krink?

Who kicked the butts of the Amphibious
Mutts?

Why, only Admiral Skink

Who's harder than a cake made of concrete?

Who's tougher than galvanised zinc?

Who's meaner and madder than a
cantankerous adder?

Why, only Admiral Skink!

Who's the galaxy's greatest dictator?

Who turns weaker despots to drink?

Who roasts rivals and traitors like burnt baked
potatoes?

Why, only Admiral Skink!

221

'Ain't we the lucky ones?' cried Sludgeclaw, pausing to regain his breath after a particularly energetic twirl. 'Old Skinky will be ever so pleased when we bring back his precious starship and the thieves what nicked it. He'll probably give us medals!'

'Medals!' cried Whiptail and all the spines on his back bristled with pleasure. 'Lovely medals!'

Sludgeclaw and Whiptail had been unable to find any rope aboard the starship, so they had taken a long string of snimploin sausages from the galley and tied their captives up with that instead. Snimploin sausages were thin and tough and had the added advantage of issuing a highly pungent smell that would keep anyone bound up by them in a constant state of mild nausea.

Sludgeclaw pushed a couple of buttons on

the control panel. 'There,' he said. 'That's our course back 'ome all plotted.'

'All plotted,' repeated Whiptail and nodded, satisfied.

'You've got to take us to Earth right now, you stupid lizard!' yelled Tori. 'An asteroid's heading right for it! We don't have long to act before it hits! You can take us to Admiral Skink – do whatever you like – afterwards! But please let us save our planet! Our home! Please?'

Sludgeclaw bent down so that his large, scaly snout was level with Tori's face. Tori grimaced and turned away, musing as she did that some enterprising tycoon could have bottled the lizard's breath and made a fortune selling it as paint stripper.

'Pay careful attention, you revolting ape,' rumbled Sludgeclaw. 'I'm gonna give yer a

223

little demonstration. Whippy? Would you be so kind as to pass my lunch?'

'Yeah, sure!' cried Whiptail and picked up one of two transparent plastic containers that were lying on the control panel. He passed it to his friend. 'Here you go, Sludgeclaw.'

'Thank you, mate,' said Sludgeclaw. He peeled off the box's lid and removed what looked to Tori like a single ordinary-looking grape – shiny and juicily blue-green. Sludgeclaw held it up daintily between his clawed thumb and forefinger.

'Here we have one stippleberry,' he said. He placed it on the floor in front of Tori with exaggerated care. The little berry looked soft and oddly vulnerable there on the starship's cold metal floor. 'Now,' said Sludgeclaw,

'I want you to imagine that this stippleberry is your planet. Earth, wasn't it? Right?'

Tori shrugged as best she was able beneath her sausage bindings. 'Okay.'

'And now,' Sludgeclaw continued, 'I want you to imagine that my fist is the asteroid what is headin' for it. You with me?'

Tori nodded grimly.

With a repulsive grunt, Sludgeclaw slammed the side of his fist on to the stippleberry. The tiny fruit exploded with a faint popping noise and sprayed its fleshy blue-green contents in all directions. Tori let out a scream. Whiptail pointed at the pulped fruit and giggled maniacally.

'That's what's gonna happen to your planet,' sniggered Sludgeclaw. 'So I suggest you get used to it.'

'Yeah. Get used to it,' repeated Whiptail. He clawed at his stubby snout. 'Ugh. A bit of stippleberry got on my nose.'

Sludgeclaw tapped Whiptail's skinny arm. 'Come on,' he said, settling himself into the captain's seat. 'We've got a long journey back 'ome. Let's stick the tellygoggler on.'

'Tellygoggler! Yay!' piped Whiptail and danced from foot to foot.

Sludgeclaw operated a control on the console and a huge vision screen lit up on one wall of the bridge. The pompous face of Jermyk Swinegum appeared.

'Tonight,' said the image of Swinegum, 'we're going to be finding out which instrument of war handles better in icy conditions: the new LX5 Snowspeed Battle Tank – or a trained moose with a load of guns taped to its antlers. . .'

'Brill Stuff!' piped Whiptail. 'My favourite programme!'

'It's marvellous, innit?' agreed Sludgeclaw. 'Turn the volume, up, Whippy.'

Whiptail adjusted the tellygoggler's volume control, then the two lizards settled back in their seats, put their feet up on the console much as Wayne had done earlier, and began to eat their packed lunches, pausing every now and then to snigger at Swinegum's antics.

'I don't know what's worse,' muttered Lance. 'The world ending or having to watch this programme.'

'What are we going to do, Lance?' hissed Tori. 'I tried biting through these vile sausages but I reckon it'd take more than human teeth to get through them.'

'And Ewargi mandibles, unfortunately,'

said Philip in a melancholy voice. 'Snimploin sausages can only be chewed apart by the savage jaws of a Swerdlixian Lizard. It seems we are doomed.'

'Try not to think about it too much, dear,' said Doreen. 'You know how contemplating a horrible death always upsets you.'

'Yes, dear,' said Philip.

Lance eyed the two lizards sitting by the console warily. Sludgeclaw and Whiptail were engrossed in the tellygoggler and hadn't heard their captives talking. 'I've got one arm sort of free-ish,' he whispered to the others. 'I can't do much with it but I can feel a square metal object on the floor just behind me. Does anyone know what it is?'

'It's my electronic diary,' said Wayne. 'It fell out of my pocket when they tied us up.

It's like the one the little lizard was using just then. Sadly, it doesn't have a super-duper laser sausage-cutting feature.'

'What can it do?' asked Lance.

'Not much,' said Wayne. 'It's a diary. You put your daily schedule – your appointments and stuff – in it. Although it can communicate with other similar machines.'

'So could we use it to send a message to Whiptail's diary?'

'Nah,' said Wayne. 'Doesn't work like that. You use the communication feature to synchronise diaries. So, for instance, if we had the password to Whiptail's diary, I could synchronise it with this one so that all his appointments were the same as mine.'

'Could you indeed?' asked Lance with a smile. 'Here, take it.' With difficulty, he slid

the electronic diary with his free hand towards Wayne. Wayne reached out with his long tubular tongue and picked it up.

'Right,' said Lance. 'Here's what we do. I want you to erase all Whiptail's appointments and add one for this afternoon.'

'Gut I'll geed the gassword,' said Wayne, his tongue wrapped around the diary.

'The password?' said Lance. 'Try "Whiptail".'

On the screen, Jermyk Swinegum was cackling with laughter while one of his co-presenters, a small hapless-looking lizard, was attempting to rodeo-ride a massive green bear-like creature. The creature shook itself violently and threw the lizard from its back, after which it proceeded to maul the lizard with its enormous claws.

'Oh dear,' smirked Swinegum, 'it looks like Ridgeheart has fallen afoul of the Snarltoothed Grizloid! And if you thought that was a dismal performance, wait 'til you see his attempt at catching an Electric Wolf in the Snow Forests of Glitchen! It really was hilarious!'

An electronic alarm chirruped.

'Ooh, that's me,' said Whiptail, taking out his electronic diary and activating it. 'Must be a reminder of something I have to do.' He studied the diary. Then he frowned and looked up at Sludgeclaw. The larger lizard was staring contentedly at the screen, oblivious. Whiptail looked down at his diary and frowned again. Then he shrugged, turned the diary off and pocketed it, then stood up. 'Won't be a moment,' he said and headed for the door.

'Yeah, whatever,' mumbled Sludgeclaw, not

turning away from the screen, and shovelled a big handful of stippleberries into his mouth.

A moment passed. Sludgeclaw guffawed loudly at the sight of Jermyk Swinegum's co-presenter being chased up a tree by a weird, luminous wolf. 'Classic!' muttered Sludgeclaw to himself. 'Absolutely classic!'

The door to the bridge opened and Whiptail re-entered. He was carrying what looked like a very long French loaf.

Sludgeclaw glanced over at him. 'Still hungry, eh Whipster? Whatcha got there?'

'Zoosyfrat baguette!' said Whiptail. 'The hardest known bread in existence!'

'Coo! Lovely!' said Sludgeclaw, smacking his rubbery green lips together. 'May I sample some?'

'Be my guest!' piped Whiptail and swung

the baguette at Sludgeclaw like a staff. The larger lizard ducked just in time and the long, thin loaf swished through the air half a centimetre above his head.

'What do you think you're playin' at, you little lunatic?' demanded Sludgeclaw. 'Put that loaf down at once!'

'There's a note in my diary that says I have to knock you unconscious right now and then knock myself unconscious too,' said Whiptail. 'It's very specific. I can't remember why I wrote it but I'm sure I must have had very good reason!' He giggled crazily and swung the baguette at Sludgeclaw again. The big lizard raised his hands and backed away.

'What? Why would you do that, Whiptail? It's the stupidest thing I ever heard! Just think for one moment!'

Agenda.

1. Knock Sludgeclaw unconscious
2. Knock myself unconscious

'No time to think!' cried Whiptail. 'Only time to bash!' He swung the loaf again and this time it connected with Sludgeclaw's head. There was a loud CRRRACK! Sludgeclaw froze.

'Whippy,' he moaned feebly, 'why would you write that in your diary? It don't make a . . . single . . . bit . . . of . . . sense.'

And with that the burly lizard collapsed in a fat, scaly heap.

'That's just what I thought,' said Whiptail and thumped himself on the back of the head so hard that the loaf snapped in two. He let out a single high-pitched giggle and toppled over.

Both lizards lay spread-eagled on the floor of the bridge. Sludgeclaw began to snore.

'Wowee!' said Lance. 'That's what I call a club sandwich!'

235

Tori groaned. 'I was just about to say how brilliant you are, Lance, but after that pun I don't think I'll bother. How are we going to get free from these sausages?'

'I'm on it,' said Wayne and shot his immensely long tongue out towards Sludgeclaw and hooked it around the handle of the lizard's disintegrator pistol. Slowly, he began to drag the gun towards them.

Lance craned his neck around to see his wristwatch. 'If we turn the ship around right now, we can still make it back to Earth in time to blow up the asteroid.'

There was a bright green flash and the sausages fell away. Everyone breathed sighs of relief and stood up, stretching their stiff limbs.

Wayne threw down the pistol and made

236

a dash for the controls, operating six different levers and switches at once with various arms, legs and antennae. The engines surged with power and Lance and the others felt the starship take a sudden swerve.

'Back on course!' said Wayne. 'I've even found us some extra power by shutting down all the ship's non-vital systems. We'll be there in two shakes of a Bingerscrawp's tail.'

As the sleek black form of the starship *Dragonworm* blazed through the silent void of space, a small white form moved over the exterior of its hull. The form moved with slow, deliberate movements, patient as a limpet clinging to a rock. With infinite care, it dragged itself towards the entrance hatch. . .

A little while later, Wayne flicked a switch on the console. Brill Stuff! vanished from the tellygoggler screen and was replaced by an image of the planet Earth hanging serenely in space.

'We're home!' said Tori.

Nearby was a silvery-grey ball that Lance initially thought was the moon, but on closer inspection, he saw it lacked the moon's familiar features. With a sickening jolt, Lance realised what it was.

'That's the view directly ahead,' said Wayne. 'Asteroid Peach is only minutes away from your planet. But it's also now in range of the ship's guns.' He beckoned Lance and Tori over. 'Here,' he said, 'I've programmed in the coordinates of the asteroid into the weapons system. All you have to do is press

this button and it's gone. Over to you, guys!'

Lance and Tori gasped.

'That's it?' said Lance. 'It's so simple! Press a button and save the world!'

'Saving the world?' laughed Tori. 'That's what we do in the Knowledge Champions!'

'Warriors, please Tori. Warriors.'

'Shut up and let's press the flipping button,' said Tori.

'Together,' said Lance.

They pressed their forefingers together and moved them in a graceful arc towards the trigger button. . .

There was a hum and the bridge door suddenly slid open. Then the weapons panel on the control console exploded in a shower of green sparks.

Lance and Tori snatched away their singed fingers.

'Yowwch!'

'What on Earth–?'

All five of them spun around to see a figure standing in the doorway. It was tall and muscled, clad in a white spacesuit. The helmet's visor was down, hiding the occupant's face. Then the figure flicked a button on a panel set into one wrist and the helmet retracted into the collar of the suit, revealing the large, green, sneering face of Admiral Skink.

'Hello there,' he said cheerfully, pointing a disintegrator pistol at the group, the end still smoking from its last discharge. 'If your plans for the evening involved not dying in horrible agony, I suggest now would be the ideal time to revise them.'

CHAPTER FIFTEEN
PEACH SURPRISE

'Now don't start misbehaving or trying to overpower me or any sort of nonsense like that,' said Admiral Skink, still in his cheery and pleasant tone. 'I'd only have to disintegrate you and, I promise you, you don't want that. They say being disintegrated by a Swerdlixian energy pistol is even more painful than taking a bath in the Acid Lakes of Hespifortunam,

where the Needle-Toothed Piranha-Worms and Plutonium-Stinged Death-Tadpoles will strip your flesh to the bone if you so much as stick your big toe in. So, please, no mucking about, eh? Let's do this in style.'

He twisted a dial on the console. There was a loud hum and a wall-panel opened, from which slid out a large, comfortable-looking sofa. 'Please,' he said, gesturing to it. 'Be seated. Make yourselves at home.'

Nobody moved. Admiral Skink squeezed the trigger of his disintegrator pistol and fired a bolt of brilliant green light at the pile of discarded Snimploin sausages. They vanished instantly with a loud sizzle, leaving a surprisingly pleasant aroma in the air that reminded Lance of Cottleton's Christmas market. Admiral Skink waved the pistol again.

242

'YOU WILL SIT ON THE SOFA!'

Meekly, they sat down. It was a bit of a squeeze for two children and three Ewargi.

'You've got to help them!' cried Wayne, his spindly antennae wobbling with indignation. 'This ship's got back-up weapons. We can still destroy that asteroid!'

'Quiet, bug,' hissed Admiral Skink.

'I don't understand,' said Lance, gently moving a stray Ewargi antenna away from his face. 'Where did you come from?'

'From an egg,' said Admiral Skink. 'That's how it works with reptiles.' He laughed.

Tori groaned and nudged Lance. 'His sense of humour's worse than yours.'

'You know what I mean, Skink,' said Lance. 'How did you get onboard this spaceship?'

Admiral Skink chortled. He spread the palm

of one of his heavily-gloved claws, revealing a black circle at its centre. 'Octoslurp Vacuum Pads! The most powerful adhesive in the galaxy. Just one could stick a woolly mammoth to the ceiling. I attached myself to the outer hull of the ship before you blasted off and let myself in through the airlock. I have been with you for the entire journey.'

He pointed at the screen.

'There is your beloved planet Earth – and there, tumbling towards it with indecent haste, is the rogue asteroid that will shortly crash into it, killing every living thing upon it and severely affecting property prices.'

He poked his disintegrator pistol against

Lance's nose. Lance cringed. 'You are the interfering monkey who disrupted my attempt to conquer that insignificant crumb of a planet,' he snarled. He raised the muzzle of the pistol to Lance's forehead. 'And it was inside this repellent pink skull that I was trapped for an interminable period of time, looking out at the universe through the dull eyes of a feeble-brained ape. How disgustingly mammalian it is in there. How small. No place for an intellect such as mine! I would have been better off inhabiting the brain of Pentaxian Slop-Beetle!'

'I'm top of my class in over half my subjects,' said Lance indignantly. 'I'm pretty bright, you know. As mammals go.'

Tori pointed at the screen. The asteroid was closing in on Earth with tremendous speed.

245

'Time's running out!' she cried. 'But we can still avert the impact! If you act quickly we can still save Earth! Please, Admiral Skink!'

Admiral Skink swung the disintegrator pistol at her. 'And you. The other meddling primate! My only regret at leaving your stinking globule of a world behind was that I wouldn't be able to see your two ugly faces when it was destroyed. But now I shall have my wish!'

He seized the ship's controls and twisted the acceleration lever. The image of Asteroid Peach on the screen grew massive as the *Dragonworm* approached it.

'Watch closely, humans, and your traitorous Ewargi helpers!' he bellowed in triumph. 'You have a front row seat at a little spectacle I like to call the destruction of the planet Earth!'

'I can't look!' said Tori and put her hands over her eyes. 'I won't!'

Admiral Skink fired his disintegrator pistol at the floor, causing a loud bang and sending up a shower of green sparks. 'You will watch!' he growled. 'Or the next thing I fire this pistol at will be this worthless Ewargi grub!' He shoved the pistol against Wayne's head. 'NOW WATCH!'

Tori opened her eyes a crack. The ship was very close to Asteroid Peach now. On the screen, the asteroid's surface looked dull and featureless. It seemed to her as if Earth was about to be destroyed by a large and quite boring pebble. 'I can't believe this is happening,' she muttered. 'Everyone we know. The whole planet. All about to vanish forever.'

'Maybe not,' said Lance with a grin. 'Look!'

As Tori watched, her heart did somersaults. 'What? What the heck is going on?'

On the screen, something strange was happening to Asteroid Peach. Long, black cracks were appearing in its silvery-grey surface. The cracks were regularly spaced and had an oddly familiar, organic quality, giving the asteroid the appearance of a huge pine cone. The cracks grew wider and deeper, becoming great fissures in its surface. With a sudden graceful burst of motion, the entire asteroid unfurled itself into a wide, flat shape covered with ridges.

Tori gasped. 'It's opening! It's changing! It's—'

'It looks like some kind of . . . giant space woodlouse!' said Lance and burst out laughing. 'It wasn't an asteroid at all!'

Admiral Skink's face fell. 'No!' he bawled at the screen. 'No! No! No! That's so unfair! It was an asteroid! It was supposed to destroy the planet! Not randomly turn into a crustacean!'

High above the Earth, the giant woodlouse flexed its massive segmented body and extended a pair of antennae as long as South America. It kicked its enormous legs (of which it had fourteen) and seemed to swim in a huge, lazy circle until it was no longer headed for Earth, but instead advancing on the *Dragonworm*. Its delicate jaws (which were

the size of Greater London) opened in a long, comfortable yawn.

Tori nudged Wayne. 'What is that thing?'

'You heard him,' said the Ewargi. 'It's a giant space woodlouse.'

'But what does it do?' asked Tori.

'Dunno,' said Wayne. '*Species of the Universe Monthly* hasn't covered them yet. Let's watch, shall we?'

The unconscious forms of Sludgeclaw and Whiptail suddenly began to stir. Whiptail looked around in confusion and rubbed his head.

'Admiral Skink!' he trilled. 'We are in the honoured presence of the Grand Ruler himself! Ace!'

'Did we miss anything, O Grand Ruler?' asked Sludgeclaw.

Admiral Skink rolled his eyes. 'Oh, not much. But watch now, all of you, as I destroy first this fearsome monster and then the entire planet Earth!'

He jabbed a panel on the control console, activating the ship's back-up weapons systems and fired a plasma bolt at the space woodlouse.

'No!' cried Tori! 'That's so horribly cruel!'

'Hello?' said Admiral Skink. 'That's why I'm doing it. I'm the really evil one, remember?'

'It's not a monster!' said Lance. 'It's a creature with as much right to—'

'To be destroyed by me as any other inferior life form!' interrupted Admiral Skink.

The plasma bolt struck the space woodlouse on its vast, ridged back. There was a tiny explosion (which must actually

have been about the size of Wales) and the space woodlouse suddenly bristled, its long antennae waving furiously.

'Ha!' cried Admiral Skink. 'That got its attention!'

He was right because what the space woodlouse did next was to clamp its jaws tightly around the hull of the *Dragonworm* and snap the ship clean in two.

CHAPTER SIXTEEN
THE SOUND OF TWO HUNDRED THOUSAND SOLDIERS SIMULTANEOUSLY BLOWING A RASPBERRY

'You big scaly flipping idiot!' yelled Tori at Admiral Skink as the floor lurched beneath their feet and a cacophony of electronic alarms began to sound.

'Ah,' said Admiral Skink. 'That may possibly not have been my best idea.'

The severed front half of the starship *Dragonworm* tumbled blindly through the

void towards Earth. Emergency shutters slammed into place, sealing the breach. On the tellygoggler screen, its occupants could see the rear half wreathed in bright yellow flames as it began to burn up in the planet's atmosphere.

'That's going to happen to us if we don't do something about it, isn't it?' said Lance.

'Yup,' said Wayne grimly.

Admiral Skink studied a read-out on the console. 'Only one escape pod left functioning. More than enough for me!' He turned to the others. 'I'm terribly sorry but it seems I must take my leave of you now. I wish you all a painful, fiery death. B'bye!' He bolted for the door.

'But what about Whippy an' me?' called Sludgeclaw.

Admiral Skink's voice echoed from down

254

the corridor. 'You pair stay behind and guard the prisoners, eh? Cheers!'

Sludgeclaw and Whiptail took out their disintegrator pistols and pointed them at the children and the Ewargi.

'Don't be a pair of morons!' said Tori. 'Your Grand Ruler has just left you to certain death! Why don't we team up and figure out what to do?'

Sludgeclaw and Whiptail exchanged a glance.

''Ow much space do you think there is in that escape pod, Whippy?' said Sludgeclaw.

'Enough for two more life forms, I reckon,' said Whiptail. 'If it's a standard Swerdlixian model.'

Sludgeclaw nodded. 'I was thinkin' the same myself.' He turned to the others with a cheery smile. 'Change of plan!' he announced and he and the smaller lizard made a run for the

door through which Admiral Skink had just left. Once it had slammed shut behind them, there came a loud crackle of energy.

Wayne tried the door.

'Gah! They've welded it shut with their disintegrator pistols!'

'Is that it?' said Tori. 'No hope?'

'There must be something we can do,' replied Lance. 'Or maybe the bit of the ship we're in could survive entering the atmosphere without burning up?'

'And then what?' said Tori. 'It smashes into the ground at a thousand miles an hour. It's like we've become an asteroid ourselves!'

'It would be ironic if it wasn't so utterly tragic,' said Philip. He and the other Ewargi laughed.

'I'm glad some people can

see the funny side of this,' said Lance and tried pushing a few buttons on the console, searching desperately for some ship's feature or piece of information that might help them. Already, the temperature in the bridge had risen dramatically and the metal control panels were nearly too hot to touch. 'It's no good,' he muttered. 'There's nothing we can do.'

'So this is it?' said Tori. 'The end?'

Lance nodded. 'It looks very much like it.'

He and Tori looked at each other in silence for a moment. Both seemed to be searching for the right words.

The sound of loud Ewargi laughter snapped them out of their contemplation.

'Oh, what is it with you three?' said Tori. 'I thought Lance was bad enough for ruining the moment but you Ewargi—'

257

'Human Beings!' laughed Doreen. 'Ain't they adorable!'

'This is a serious moment, you bunch of brainless beetles!' said Lance. 'We're all going to die!'

Wayne shook his head. 'No,' he said. 'We're not.'

'What? How come?'

'We Ewargi are hardy little creatures,' said Wayne. 'We can go for ages without oxygen; we can withstand radiation, and our shells are even tough enough to survive the heat of atmospheric entry.'

'Well that's fine for you,' said Lance. 'I don't know if they mentioned it in *Species of the Universe Monthly,* but Human Beings can't do any of those things. You lot might survive but Tori and I are definitely going to die!'

'No, you're not,' said Wayne. 'Because another thing we Ewargi can do is this . . . '

With a sound like clingfilm being rolled away from its cardboard tube, Wayne and his parents suddenly stretched and elongated their bodies until they became much wider and extremely flat. It was as if they had been pressed like flowers between the pages of some immense book. Lance and Tori looked on in puzzlement. The three flattened Ewargi folded themselves around each other, forming a large, hollow ball. A gap opened up in it.

'Climb in,' said Wayne. 'Go on. You'll be quite safe. I promise.'

The children obeyed.

'Here we go,' said Wayne. 'Hang on to your hats. Next stop, Earth!'

Within the darkness of the Ewargi sphere, Lance and Tori could hear the remains of the *Dragonworm* being torn apart around them by the fierce forces of atmospheric entry. At one point the starship's artificial gravity generator must have been destroyed because Lance and Tori suddenly found themselves floating.

'Zero gravity!' said Tori, gently rotating. 'Brilliant!'

'I don't think it agrees with me,' said Lance, clutching his stomach as he tumbled head over heels. 'I feel like a sock in a washing machine.'

'Some space traveller you are!'

'If I die of space nausea,' said Lance, 'I want you to have my laptop so you can continue the work of the Knowledge Warriors. The password is–'

'I know what it is,' said Tori. 'I guessed it. It's "Sally", isn't it?'

Lance nodded sheepishly, glad that in the darkness Tori couldn't see his reddening cheeks. 'How did you guess?'

Tori grinned. 'It's obvious.'

'Guys,' said Wayne, his voice sounding weirdly warbly within the insect shell sphere, 'we're almost through the Earth's atmosphere. We'll be landing shortly. Whereabouts on the planet do you need to be?'

'It's a place called Hyde Park,' said Lance. 'In London.'

'Ah!' said Wayne. 'That'll be the capital city of the United Kingdom of Great Britain and Northern Ireland, then?'

'Bang on!' said Lance. 'What excellent service! But tell me one thing. . .'

261

'Yes?' said Wayne.

'How do you land? I should imagine we're falling at quite a speed. Have you got some kind of parachute thing or something?'

'No,' said Wayne. 'We fire our retro rockets. You know, in the opposite direction. Slows us down nicely.'

'You have retro rockets?' said Lance incredulously. 'An insect species that's evolved retro rockets?'

'Well,' said Wayne, 'We call them retro rockets.'

'What are they really, then?'

'Our bottoms.'

'Your–?'

262

'Hang on!' said Wayne. 'Prepare for landing!'

Imagine an army. Imagine two hundred thousand big, burly soldiers all standing silently at attention. Now imagine a general standing on a high balcony looking down at the army. The army are waiting for his signal. The general checks his watch, counting down . . . three . . . two . . . and now he lowers his hand with a dramatic sweeping gesture. At that signal, every one of the soldiers sticks out his tongue and blows a raspberry – producing the loudest, longest, wettest, thunderiest raspberry imaginable. Well, the Ewargi 'retro rockets' sounded pretty much like that. Fortunately for Lance and Tori, the force of the noise was projected down at the ground and away from them.

After a time, the thunderous raspberry

subsided and the two children felt the Ewargi sphere judder to a halt.

'I am happy to announce,' said Wayne, 'that we have made a perfect touchdown in the centre of the wonderful Earth city of London. Please wait one moment before disembarking while I and my mum and dad unroll ourselves.'

Tori pounced on Lance and gave him an enormous hug. 'We're home! We did it!'

Lance blushed and disengaged himself. 'I know. I can't quite believe we're actually here.'

The three Ewargi made their clingfilm noise and the hollow ball suddenly split into three parts. Lance and Tori found themselves deposited in the middle of a busy city pavement, surrounded by a lot of very confused-looking people. Wayne, Doreen and Philip shook themselves and waved their

limbs and antennae until they had resumed their usual forms. Seeing this extraordinary sight, several people screamed, and then, when nothing much happened afterwards, walked away feeling slightly foolish.

Lance and Tori looked around. Lance noticed a very tall structure looming over the surrounding buildings. He frowned at it. 'You know how I said I couldn't quite believe you could take us to London?' He jerked a thumb at the tall structure. 'Well, we're not! That's the Eiffel Tower!'

'Wayne!' laughed Tori. 'You've landed in the wrong country! I thought you knew about the planet Earth!'

Wayne shrugged. 'Never said I was an expert, did I?'

CHAPTER SEVENTEEN
STOCKS AND SHARES

A rotten cabbage sailed through the air with the grace of a dove and exploded with an evil-smelling squelch against the Prime Minister's forehead. It was followed by three tomatoes, a plastic tray of cold chips and half a thick, gooey milkshake.

The Prime Minister sighed as the thick, pink goo ran down his glasses. 'Fine, fine,'

he called. 'Go ahead. Have your fun.'

'We will!' cried a voice in the crowd and unleashed a fresh hail of rotten foodstuffs.

Some enterprising soul with a knowledge of history had raided a nearby museum and pinched a set of sixteenth-century punishment stocks – a pair of large, hinged wooden boards on a heavy wooden stand. The boards had holes in for a person's head and hands and the idea was that you trapped your victim inside and allowed whoever happened to be around at the time to dole out whatever punishment they felt was appropriate. This usually took the form of heaving a bunch of rotten fruit and vegetables at the luckless prisoner, to the hilarity of all who watched.

Mrs Spratley had been first in the queue.

The furious swishing of helicopter blades filled the air again. Mr and Mrs Spratley looked up and saw another large military helicopter, this one bearing a French flag insignia. The aircraft hovered briefly near the temporary stage built to house the omega wave projector, sending a few people scattering, and brought itself down on to the grass in a slow, stately manner.

Two children and three large insect-creatures climbed out. The helicopter sounded a hooter a couple of times and then took off again. Mr and Mrs Spratley stared at the five figures in wonder. The white-coated scientists put down their rulers and notebooks.

PC Sledge clicked his fingers. 'Ewargi! I bet they're Ewargi!' he announced in a smug voice

– but sadly no one was within earshot to be impressed by his knowledge.

One of the insect-creatures opened its mandibles and made a sound like an outboard motor discovering it had just won the National Lottery.

'As you haven't had the benefit of telepathic ice cream,' said Lance to those watching, 'allow me to translate on behalf of our three friends here. We're very happy to be here on planet Earth! Especially as it's not now going to be destroyed by Asteroid Peach!'

'Isn't it?' called a stray voice from the crowd.

'Why? What's happened?' called another voice.

'Look in the sky,' called a third in surprise. 'It's gone!'

'Oh,' said a fourth, adding, somewhat anticlimactically, 'good.'

'You mean you hadn't noticed?' said Lance.

'It slipped our minds in all the hoo-ha,' said a fifth.

Tori shook her head. 'A rogue asteroid transforms itself into a giant space woodlouse right in front of your eyes and you don't even notice?'

'Get off our backs!' called a sixth voice from the crowd. 'It's been a very weird couple of days!' Other crowd members voiced their agreement.

Lance shrugged at the Ewargi. 'I apologise for my species. Sometimes we can be a little short-sighted.'

'No worries, mate,' laughed Wayne.

'Have you got the floobledoop plant or

270

whatever it's called, Lance?' asked Mrs Spratley. 'The stuff to make this purple beast sneeze and free your sister?'

'Certainly have, Mum,' said Lance and put his hand in his pocket. His face turned white. 'Oh no,' he said. 'It's not here! I must have lost it when we were struggling with Sludgeclaw and Whiptail!'

'It's okay,' said Wayne, slipping his hand into one of his own pockets. 'I'm sure I've got a little left over. Ah. Oh dear.'

'What?' said Lance.

Wayne drew out his hand and opened it. It was filled with powdery grey-black ash. 'It must have burned up when we were entering your planet's atmosphere. Sorry.'

'So we risked our lives travelling to another galaxy to find some flooblescoop plant and we haven't got any left at all?' said Tori, her face falling.

'Oh, no,' said Wayne. 'And I don't suppose it's very likely that you'll be able to find a similar substance on this world that's a disaccharide molecule with the chemical formula $C12H22O11$?' said Wayne. 'Pretty slim odds, I should think.'

'A disaccharide molecule with the chemical formula $C_{12}H_{22}O_{11}$?' repeated Tori. 'I'm afraid I wouldn't know where to start.'

Lance turned very red. He looked at his parents and saw the sorrow and disappointment in their eyes. That was too much to bear so he looked down at the ground instead, his whole body burning with shame. He might have saved the planet from destruction, but he'd failed to rescue his little sister. The world seemed to contract around him and it felt as if time were standing still, stretching out this awful moment into infinity.

'It's sugar,' said a quiet voice.

'What?' said Lance, looking up.

'The chemical you need to make the creature sneeze. It's ordinary sugar.'

273

Everyone looked around to see who had spoken – and were astonished to find it was the Prime Minister.

Lance and Tori ran up to the stocks and released him. The Prime Minister ran a hand through his milkshake-soaked hair. 'Thank you,' he said, wiping his glasses on his tie. 'I studied chemistry at university, you see. Organic chemistry, to be precise. Before I got mixed up in politics. It's definitely sugar you need.'

'Where can we get some?' asked Lance.

The Prime Minister put his hand in his pocket and produced a key. He handed it to Lance. 'There's a cupcake in the glove compartment of my car – that big Rolls-Royce parked behind the stage. That should do the trick.'

The white-coated scientists stood in front of the giant purple lizard-creature. Holding a large net that they had removed from a football goal in another part of the park.

Lance Spratley, watched by his parents, his friend Tori Walnut, and the Prime Minister of the United Kingdom of Great Britain and Northern Ireland, removed a small yellow cupcake from its paper wrapping and crumbled it in his hands. The Prime Minister sighed to see a good cupcake go to waste, but then he remembered what it was being used for, and, to his utter astonishment, he found himself starting to smile. He hadn't tried to smile at all; it had just occurred spontaneously when he thought about how he was helping people.

It felt good.

Lance poured the cupcake crumbs into the nostrils of the dozing lizard-creature. It made a sudden, startled sniffing noise and opened wide its two enormous eyes.

'It's happening!' yelled Lance. 'Take cover!' He and the others ran to safety, leaving the scientists holding the net quaking in front of the lizard-creature like a wall of footballers facing a free kick at close range.

The lizard-creature reared back its head, spluttered once or twice, closed its eyes – and then, with a sound like a hurricane passing through a custard factory, expelled a gargantuan quantity of air and viscous reptilian snot from its nose and mouth. Sally Spratley shot out amongst the goo and landed in the centre of the net.

The scientists let out a cheer and placed

the little girl gently on the ground.

'Ha!' cried Sally, jumping to her feet. 'That was fun! Again! Again!'

That night, a feast was held at 10 Downing Street. The guests of honour were a pair of children, their families and a trio of alien insects. Fizzy pop was drunk in great quantities. Small mountains of crisps were hoovered up by hungry mouths. And a great

many specially baked cupcakes were consumed. The cupcakes bore a commemorative design etched into their icing. It was meant to show Lance and Tori stepping into the omega wave projector but due to a mix-up at the baker's, all the cakes arrived topped with a drawing of a pig and the words *Happy 5th Birthday Porky Sue!* No one seemed to mind, however, as the cakes themselves were delicious.

A small pigtailed figure carrying a plate threaded her way through the celebrating guests and approached Lance and Tori, who were sitting near the end of a long dining table, sipping pop and talking

excitedly about their adventures. Lance looked up.

'Hi, Sally! What have you got there?'

'It's for you, Lance,' said Sally in a shy little voice. 'I wanted to say thank you for getting me out of the monster's insides and also for risking your life saving the whole wide world. It really was extra super brave. So I got the chef to make a sandwich just for you. It's got sausages and bacon and mustard and ketchup and cress and crisps in it. All your favourite things. I wanted you to have it because you're my favouritest brother.'

'Oh, how thoughtful!' said Tori.

'Wowee,' said Lance in a soft voice. 'Thank you, Sally. Thank you very much. You're my favouritest sister.'

279

He took the sandwich off the plate and sank his teeth into it. A second later he grimaced and spat it out into a napkin.

'Ugh! This sandwich is full of soil! I think I'm going to be sick!'

'Ha!' cried Sally. 'Tricked you, loser!' and skipped away.

EPILOGUE

Somewhere in the Australian Outback...

The town of Woolamagonga Springs wasn't really a town at all. It was just a few tired-looking shacks huddled together for mutual shade in the sun's pitiless glare. Had you been flying over the place in an aeroplane and looked down, you would probably have thought it was a speck of dirt on the window. The natural water springs that had given this desert settlement its name had long since dried up, and along with it, the principal reason why anyone would ever choose it as a place to visit.

The old swagman limped along the dirt road as fast as his aching feet and sole-flapping

281

boots could carry him. His hair was fluffy and snow white and perched lightly on his head like a hat made out of cloud. The swagman pushed open the door of a large white clapboard building with a clatter, sending a lazing cat yowling off down the road, and bustled his way into its main office.

Jobie Jones, who was Woolamagonga Springs's chief law enforcement officer, town mayor, postmaster, shopkeeper and fireman, looked up from his morning newspaper in astonishment at the breathless, panting figure of the old swagman standing before him.

'Blimey! What's up, mate?'

'They're coming!' cried the old swagman in a hoarse, terrified voice. 'Take cover! Run away! Hide! They're coming, I tell you!'

'Who's coming, mate? I've just put a pot of

coffee on, by the way. Would you care to join me in a cup? There's some croissants over there by the photocopier too.'

'No time for coffee!' cried the swagman. 'No time for croissants! They are nearly upon us! Destruction is at hand!'

Jobie Jones put his newspaper down on the desk in front of him. 'Who's coming, mate? You sound kinda shaken up if you don't mind me saying.'

'Invaders!' cried the swagman. 'Soldiers!'

Jobie Jones frowned. 'What's that? Invading soliders? Coming here to Woolamagonga Springs? Are you sure you have that right, mate?'

'I've seen them!' said the swagman. 'I saw them out on the road. They're headed this way! They're bringing death and destruction,

283

I can tell!'

'What do they look like, these soldiers?'

'There's three of them. Two big ones and a little one. All in green they are! And ugly as crocodiles! There's evil in their hearts. Mark my words!'

Jobie Jones picked up his newspaper and started to read it again. 'I wouldn't worry too much about that, mate,' he said in a friendly tone. 'Sounds like you've been out in the sun a bit too long, that's all. The heat plays tricks on the old brainbox. That and all the stuff in the papers about asteroids and woodlice and heaven knows what else. People's imaginations run away with them these days. Come on. Have a seat, mate. The croissants really are very good today.'

The old swagman sat down heavily and

looked at the tray of croissants. 'Maybe you're right, mate,' he said, his breath slowly returning. He wiped his forehead with the back of his hand. 'I been out in that sun a long time. I musta made some kind of mistake. It was probably just some backpackers all got up in that camouflage gear they wear.'

'Yeah, probably was, mate.'

The swagman picked up a croissant. His mouth began to water. It had been a long time since he'd eaten. . .

Then he heard singing. It was coming from outside. Three loud, raucous singing voices

Who slew the Treeshrews of Vega?
Who conquered the Ice Wolves of Krink?
Who kicked the butts of the Amphibious
  Mutts?

There was a loud bang and the door to the office suddenly exploded in a shower of green sparks. Jobie Jones and the swagman screamed in unison and dived behind the desk for cover. They peeped over and saw three dark figures standing silhouetted in the doorway, against the blinding sunlight.

The smallest of the figures let out a trilling, high-pitched giggle.